# Light
# Stealer

## James Barclay

Introduction by Stan Nicholls

*PS Publishing, 2002*

## ISBN
## 1 902 880 61 7 (Softback)
## 1 902 880 62 5 (Hardback)

**PS Publishing LLP**
Hamilton House
4 Park Avenue
Harrogate HG2 9BQ
ENGLAND

### e-mail
crowth1@attglobal.net

### Internet
http://www.pspublishing.co.uk

*This special signed edition*
*is limited to:*

*500 numbered paperback copies*
*and*
*300 numbered hardcover copies.*

*This is copy* ...43...

# INTRODUCTION

AN editor with one of the major publishers once told me they would love to see all novels produced in plain wrappers, bearing only the title, author name and a brief synopsis. No indication of genre, no jacket illustration to hint at the kind of fiction on offer.

It was irony, of course. This editor didn't seriously believe such a thing would ever happen, and certainly wasn't implying writers should be ashamed of their chosen genre. After all, everything's genre, even so-called mainstream literature; it just happens to be the one that lays claim to cultural superiority. No, this editor was railing at *categorisation*, the system of pigeonholing books by type that allows literary snobs to sneer at fiction they perceive as inferior. More important, labelling a book by genre is a green light to preconceptions and prejudices, often uninformed, that can steer a potential reader away from a rewarding, entertaining, even enlightening experience.

The categories that have suffered most from this bigotry are fantasy and its offshoot, science fiction. Sf's travails are well documented, and although intolerance of it lingers to some extent - most of us working in these areas still get asked when we're going to write something *serious* - its history can be seen as a slow climb to respectability. Science fiction as a recognisably discrete form is surprisingly young, most scholars placing its emergence in the 1920s. The interesting thing about fantasy as we've come to know it, ie as a packaged genre, is that it's even younger, dating from as recently as the 1960s. That's a paradox, because fantasy has always been with us. It's the oldest expression of the human imagination, from the fanciful tales of gods and wondrous creatures told by our ancient ancestors, via the *Odyssey* and *Beowulf*, to the amazing myth-weaving of Tolkien.

I won't attempt a definition of fantasy here. (Though when I worked in a science fiction bookshop in London's Soho I had some very engaging conversations about what fantasy might be with numerous men in grubby overcoats. But that's another story.) The fact that you're reading this book confirms you're adept at knowing fantasy when you see it. And a person with extremely good taste, I might add. As you're probably an aficionado, you'll be aware that fantasy has suffered the same sort of disdain that plagued sf for so many years. Arguably more so, as some of its detractors live in the ghetto next door - sf fans, who should know better, are want to complain about fantasy's lack of scientific rigour in respect of the magical systems and mythical beasts it depicts. Yeah, and faster than light drives, telepathy and time travel are scientifically verifiable.

But here's the good news. Fantasy is coming of age. We don't have to be embarrassed or defensive about it anymore. Part of its growing acceptance is down to Pratchett, Rowling and a superb film adaptation of *The Lord of the Rings*, granted. But even before these phenomena the field was displaying confidence, zest and signs of a fresh maturity, thanks to a new young breed of fantasy writers.

English author James Barclay is prominent in their ranks. His impressive debut, *Dawnthief*, beginning the Chronicles of the Raven, picked up the kind of notices and reader response any first-timer would envy. Subsequent novels *Noonshade*, *Nightchild* and *Elfsorrow* have consolidated his status as a skilful and imaginative storyteller, an original talent applying himself with gusto to exotic, fantastical action adventures.

*Light Stealer* is a treat. Set in Balaia, a land already familiar to Barclay's readers, it tells of Septern, a master mage teaching at Dordover college. A man whose vanity is only outstripped by his naiveté, Septern's most abiding passion is magic. Mind freed by a surfeit of alcohol (a writerly device if ever I heard one), he achieves his ambition to create the ultimate spell, Dawnthief. This is the doomsday spell which, if cast, would deprive the world of light and air, condemning all living things to suffer "perpetual dark and perfect vacuum." Septern devises it not to use, but to prove it's possible. (A parallel here with the way some scientists think.) Oblivious to the war ravaging Balaia, he decides to travel to a conclave of mages and announce his great discovery. For all his genius, Septern is less worldly than his four youthful students, Janeth, Dirrion, Sandor and Thuneron. They can see, where he can't, that making the existence of Dawnthief public will attract the attention of every warring army, friend or foe. And for a prize so awesome any price is worth paying. But the mage's arrogance blinds him to the danger, leaving his inexperienced apprentices to face the onslaught.

There's an excellent twist I don't think you're going to see coming. The mechanics of the magic sound really plausible (at least as much as FTL drives, telepathy and time travel), the characters are pithily drawn, the dialogue's crisp, there's a natural flow of wit. *Light Stealer* not only entertains, it defies expectations, as all good fiction should.

What you have here, oh reader who cares not to wrap their book in a brown paper bag lest it offends, is the work of a fabulist in a fine imaginative tradition. A scion of Morris, Dunsany, Eddison, Howard, Leiber, De Camp, Vance, LeGuin, Moorcock, Jordan, Brooks, Eddings, Feist and Gemmell. Even if he is devoted to football (sport or exercise of any kind being anathema to most writers), James Barclay is a writer to watch, and this volume something to treasure.

And if the literati prefer *The Collected Laundry Lists of Virginia Wolfe* volume III, that's their loss.

*Stan Nicholls*
*August 2002*

# Light Stealer

# Chapter 1

IT HAD BEEN simple, really. Most fundamental magic was, when you looked at its roots. The problem, when experimenting with fundamentals, was seeing through the complexities of conditioning to the blindingly obvious. And not dying in the process.

For Septern, nominally of the mage college of Dordover, clear sight had come when he was sprawling blind drunk across his dining room table.

He had decided to eat alone that night. An unusual decision but one he was later to look back on as prophetic. Usually, he encouraged his students to dine with him. He enjoyed the debate, it inspired thought and gave birth to creation – the life blood of a mage's trade.

But he had been in an off mood all that day. He couldn't close his mind on anything and he'd felt there was something just escaping his consciousness. Whatever, it had made him irritable, the day's research had not gone well and all four of his charges had disappeared to their rooms. He had not invited them to the dining room.

Septern had gone for a walk around his grounds with a glass and a bottle of red from the fledgling but very promising Blackthorne vineyards. He had felt sorry for them in a way. In one respect his students were lucky. Hand-picked from the Dordovan intake to learn from his acknowledged genius – and he but thirty years older than them.

But the fast-track to Dordovan Master Mage status had its price. And these four earnest young men were paying that price now.

The honour of studying at the Septern Manse carried them on a cloud of late adolescent ego for a few days. But then reality set in. The Manse was in the middle of nowhere, two days from the nearest settlement of any appreciable size. And young men wanted female company. His cook wasn't up to it – not for thirty years by the looks of her – and he couldn't even boast any maids. There had been trouble before so part of the student discipline now was to keep the Manse clean.

Septern had made his choice two decades earlier. Something about the genesis of new magic fulfilled him like no relationship he had ever experienced. He'd never seen it in another mage, and certainly not in this current crop. Septern supposed that was what sent him apart from other mages. *All* other mages. Many were clever, some were gifted, but all were distracted, man or woman, by what drove them at the most basic human level.

Not Septern. What drove *him* was creation of magic. That was purity and nothing else came even close. And the wonders he had seen and the places he had travelled made the sacrifice worthwhile. None of them would ever understand, not fully. That was what made him different. Better.

And so, while his students had sat alone, or together in their rooms, talking their nonsense and dreaming their dreams of anything but magic, Septern had completed his walk, uncorked a second bottle and drunk himself slowly but surely to incoherence. It was a stupor the beautifully tender beef had done nothing to mitigate.

That night, though, the alcohol had freed his subconscious mind and the secrets he craved had been presented to him. Every night since his awakening in the Dordovan Mana Bowl, he'd dreamed of originating the ultimate spell. That night, it happened.

It was the chill puddle of vomit under his cheek, though, that had woken him to the enormity.

)(

Janeth remembered Septern that morning as resembling a man in the last stages of dementia. A spitting madman, hair matted in beef gravy, vomit caking his cheek, robes stained and filthy where he'd pulled his uneaten supper into his lap.

Words tripped from his mouth in a galloping babble, his arms had minds of their own, gesturing, pointing and beckoning, and his legs propelled him in what was at best a controlled fall.

But the mago's eyes gave the lie to every other part of his body and appearance. They shone with a fervour Janeth had already come to recognise in his few months of study. The naked energy that indicated Septern had discovered something. And by the looks of him that morning, it was something extraordinary.

The main laboratory, which let off the back of the entrance hall had been quiet since Janeth and his three colleagues had entered at dawn. Aileen, the rake-thin grey haired cook, had intercepted them at the door to the dining room to tell them breakfast would be served in the kitchen. The master, she had said rather bizarrely, had not yet finished his supper.

Over the weeks and months, they had seen a dozen idiosyncrasies in Septern's manner but this was something else, even for him. But, as they'd learned to do, they had shrugged their shoulders, broken their fast and gone back to their books, manashape plots and stability tests.

It had been shortly before mid-morning, during the test of the full shape of an enhanced vermin-repellent wide-area ward (something their tutor considered painfully simple) that Septern had crashed in. Moments later, the course of the future turned down a new and ultimately far bloodier path.

Janeth was the acknowledged leader and spokesman of the students. He was nineteen, bespectacled and very tall, with a brain that delivered manashapes with great efficiency. His problem, and one he hoped to solve through his time with Septern, was concentration in distracting circumstances. He wanted to be a mage capable of casting in a hurricane and the heat of battle, on a storm-tossed ship and in the middle of a market crowd.

And so he stood, implacable as Septern had taught him, while his master delivered his spittle-strewn comments . . . not one of which made an ounce of sense.

'Well?' demanded Septern when he saw none of them move so much as a muscle.

'Two things,' said Janeth, holding up two fingers and bearing in mind that Septern called confidence the right hand of concentration. 'First, slow down: tell us again and we'll be happy to assist, Master Septern. Second, while we're assembling what you need, please wash and change.'

'No time, no time,' snapped Septern. 'You don't understand.' He stepped forward and gripped Janeth's arms. The stench of vomit and sweat was overpowering. 'I have found it. No spell will be greater. No spell. Don't you see?'

His eyes searched Janeth's face, their energy almost too bright to bear. 'Janeth, we are at the summit. All we have to do is claim it for ourselves.'

Janeth nodded. 'Master Septern, I can see you've discovered something. And I can see there is work for us to do. But one of your lessons is to minimise distractions during research; and right now, you look terrible and smell worse. So issue your instructions then go and bathe or you'll distract us. Really.'

Janeth felt the lab tense. Septern wasn't used to being challenged or directed on anything. He would take this one of two ways. Janeth prepared for the storm.

Septern glared at him for a few heartbeats. Enough to make him very uneasy and the sweat begin to bead on his forehead. Then he patted Janeth's neck with a cupped hand.

'That's why I like you,' he said, breathing deep, smiling and dispelling the tension. 'You don't fear and that is a critical quality. All right, here's what I need.

'The manastream charts we constructed following the testing of the DuskFall spell; the geometric model of HellFire; Arteche's texts on application of base lore to modulating constructs; my previous work on the potential sentience of magic and anything you can find regarding the nature of air inside a freely expanding mana construct.

'And you, Janeth,' he concluded, placing a grimy hand briefly on the young student's chest. 'I need you to construct the modulating tetrahedron at the core of a HellFire and monitor its decay until I return. Got all that?'

A chorus of affirmatives greeted the question. Septern nodded.

'I'll be back very soon. No time to waste.'

He strode to the lab door, looking back over his shoulder as he grasped the handle.

'You do understand, of course that all this is merely by way of smoothing the edges. I already know I'm right.'

Janeth turned to see his friends' bemused expressions.

'What the hell was all that about?' asked Dirrion, short, freckled, nervous and brilliant.

'I'm not sure but I think things are about to change.' Janeth's heart was already beating faster.

♓

Septern could barely concentrate on the basics. Even walking upstairs was a trial which bruised his knees. Later, he'd thank Aileen for laying out fresh clothes and having drawn a hot bath but at the time, it was all he could do to strip and splash. He never stopped to consider what he would have done if nothing had been prepared.

As it was, his mind stole his concentration and his hair remained unbrushed and his shirt was cross-buttoned. His shoe buckles were loose and his collar turned under. He blew back into the lab, a piece of bread forgotten in his hand.

'Well?' he demanded, snapping the fingers of his free hand. 'Is everything ready for review?'

'Yes, Master Septern,' they chorused, nervousness on every face. For a moment he craved to be one of them. To be in his presence waiting for his next utterance. He wondered what it felt like to hear the genius rather than create it. Just for a moment.

He smiled. 'Don't worry. In fact, be ready for glory. You are about to participate in the most important day in spell creation history.'

'Can we know what is it you have discovered, Master Septern?' asked Sandor, a student with the physique of a warrior and the brain of a master mage. His was a face that would break a thousand hearts.

Septern shook his head. 'Not just like that.'

He regarded them all while inside, his body buzzed and his blood surged with the excitement. He was fighting hard to keep control of the discipline he had to practice now of all times – after all, it had been he who had laid the new rules of check and balance every college now operated.

Do what you demand of others, he instructed himself.

Well, mostly.

'Let me educate you,' continued Septern, spreading his arms wide. 'That is, after all, why you are here. We will check and pace, we will discuss and balance. And you will tell me what it is I have discovered. And believe me, your names will forever be connected with greatness.'

'Connected?' queried Janeth.

Septern smiled. 'There are many who's efforts are crucial but there can only ever be one creator.'

♓

Janeth watched for the rest of the day and tried to hate the man for whom he had been asked to give up any semblance of normal life. Of course he worked, he fetched, read, experimented, questioned and answered. But he watched like the others didn't. In his mind, he challenged the ego that could make such statements but, when all was said and done, everything Septern said was right. Arrogance or supreme confidence? Neither. Genius. It made its own rules and normal man had no conception of how it felt.

'So,' said Septern, turning to Sandor. It was late afternoon. The shadows were beginning to lengthen and plates of half eaten food lay strewn across the work surfaces, holding down pages and parchments. 'Dirrion has just read a passage that concludes what?'

There was a pause. Janeth felt scared for him. These were not questions you wanted. Neither could you afford to answer them incorrectly.

'That a – well, that potentially, that a self-sustaining construct can, potentially, exclude air within itself as it expands.'

'Potentially?' demanded Septern.

Sandor's eyes stabbed left and right but no help was forthcoming. 'Yes. No one has yet proved the theory. Therefore we may only assume potential.'

'Excellent.' Septern's eyes covered them all. 'Never assume unproven actuality. Potential is as dangerous as it is exciting. A very

14

difficult child. Now, Thuneron, the measurements we extrapolated from the body of results on the DuskFall spell suggest it can expand once released by a mage, yes?'

'Yes,' confirmed Thuneron, nodding the mass of curly brown hair that topped his narrow pale face.

'No!' Septern thumped the table at his right hand. 'Think harder. Again, but be quick.'

Thuneron's hands rubbed nervously along his thighs. Janeth could all but hear his mind flicking back over the pages, grasping to recall the critical fault Septern wanted.

'The lore exists within the construct for limited expansion...' He hesitated. Septern tutted. Thuneron snapped his fingers. 'Got it. The decay rate figures showed an acceleration. The lore is flawed for a casting as large as Master Hoeth suggests is possible. The spell would collapse. Not dangerously, but it would collapse before reaching critical size.'

'So,' said Septern nodding his approval at Thuneron. 'We have a flow and some fascinating potential but we have no goal. And, more than that, we have no control. Not yet.'

'And what can we infer?' asked Dirrion.

Another nod from Septern. 'A good question. So far, I have given you precious little yet you have learned considerably more. It is all about assimilation of ideas, thoughts and facts. That's it. We have summed up mage learning in an instant.

'But we are left unfocused. We need an aim. And here, there are no wrong answers. Only opinions plus my desires. Check me and challenge me. It's so simple, we have all missed it so far.'

Septern stood up and walked around the back of his chair. Janeth could feel a classic oration coming on. He was not to be disappointed.

'Magic is a dud word and concept. It implies chance, coincidence and wonder. Spell development is none of these things. It requires application, diligence and a spark.' He flicked the side of his head with an index finger. 'And I'll teach you how to free your minds to spark, don't worry.

'What I have given you and what you have heard today is the application. What comes now is the spark. Listen closely, this is good stuff.

'A stable DuskFall spell could cover an area perhaps the size of Dordover, the City itself, not just the college. Its shape is already well-designed and there is no doubt it would dim the sun above it. Clever, but irrelevant. What we are interested in here is the lore of the construct. And what we have to add is an element that will allow the shape to self-sustain *and* to continue expanding.'

Septern paused. Janeth felt the atmosphere. Such an element or lore fragment didn't exist to his knowledge. At least, not yet. Septern's eyes burned and his mouth held a slight smile. No doubt he was desperate both that one of his students would grasp what he was theorising and that none of them would – to allow him to announce whatever it was as a genius alone. His conceit was certainly great enough. Something lurked in the back of Janeth's mind. He knew a question was coming his way and it would be all to do with the decay graph of the shape he had constructed and monitored.

'But merely to produce a self-sustaining and expanding shape is worthless if it does not complete a purpose,' said Septern. 'And I have long had a purpose in mind. All I didn't have was the spark. Now I have it.

'Tell me, Janeth, the HellFire tetrahedron you built. Its decay model. What did you notice?'

Janeth felt himself smiling. He knew he was going to give the right answer. 'It didn't decay. In the end I had to dismiss it. That fragment was looking perpetual. I'd like to have more time to study it.'

'You don't need more time. The fragment is perpetual though on its own, utterly useless. Very good.' Septern nodded. 'Very good.'

He leaned over the back of the chair, resting his arms. The room fell utterly silent. Not that it had been noisy before, but this hush had the qualities of reverence and expectation. All of them knew Septern was about to reveal what these disparate elements might produce. Janeth was sure it had nothing to do with peace and harmony. How right he was.

'So, let us conjoin our puzzle,' said Septern, savouring his moment. 'We take the HellFire tetrahedron's inherent stability and apply it to the DuskFall's manaflow model. Into this mix we place the expanding construct laws which, I can assure you, do exclude air most effectively. How do you think I know this?'

Janeth knew four blank looks were facing Septern.

'No? Because the same stability in the HellFire tetrahedron begets the core of the expansion theory. And what does the HellFire spell exclude at *its* core, so slight that only the knowledgeable have noted and monitored it?'

He surveyed them all again. 'And you Janeth, you saw it too. I guarantee it.'

Janeth nodded. He had and his mind was sending cold to play across his heart.

'Light,' he said.

Septern snapped his fingers. 'Light.' He smiled.

'But surely the lores are incompatible? Any fully functioning HellFire tetrahedron can only be operated through Xeteskian base lore,' said Thuneron.

'Correct,' said Septern. 'But two things have slipped your mind, dear student. One, I am cognizant of most Xeteskian lore, including that of the HellFire spell. Two, magic *is* sentient. You have all read my thesis. Or did you think it idle speculation?'

Janeth voiced the remaining confusion. 'Even so, Master Septern, the lore constructs of these spells cannot be spliced. They cover two colleges. It is impossible.'

'Indeed it is,' said Septern. 'And there is where the mistake is being made by us all. And it is where we must look to the more mundane to help us. As I have done.'

They were hanging on his every word and Janeth could only smile at the theatre of it all. He had dragged it out, tantalised them with possibilities and the potential of glory. The trouble was, Janeth knew that the final piece of the jigsaw, Septern's spark, was something only he would understand.

'We do not splice, as all our teaching demands. No, we bind. As we bind wounds until they heal and can grow again. As we bind squares of off-cuts to make a blanket. Splice? Why, when there is something far simpler?'

Septern tapped his head. 'Simplicity is where genius lies.'

Janeth looked at his fellow students, saw them

open-mouthed and grappling to understand. But there was something not right and it was a nag not long irritating him beyond his grasp.

'But a binding cannot grow,' he said quietly. 'By its very nature it is outside the construct. It has no life beyond its joining.'

Everyone was looking at him. Septern's face was neutral. Janeth had no choice but to carry on. 'You are suggesting a spell construct which can expand with complete stability. Yet a binding will surely restrict that. It won't work.'

Septern walked over to Janeth and stood very close to him. The room had cooled. Janeth felt nervous, unsure. He knew he was shaking but he also knew he was right. He waited for the verdict.

Septern lifted his head and his expression was serene. He laid a hand on Janeth's shoulder.

'And that is why you will attain Mage Master status in advance of your beguiled colleagues. You are a thinker.' He stepped back before continuing. 'Janeth is, of course, right. But there is, of course, more. The binding shall be the sentient part of the spell. It shall have the ability to evolve, to grow. And if you give mana the raw materials, it will do your bidding. It will find a way.'

And there is was, just as Janeth knew. That piece only Septern understood. The spark. Yet it was so simple even a child could grasp the basic theory. A random seed in soil will grow when the rains come and the sun shines. Remove one and the plant will die. Otherwise, the plant could become anything. Potential realised. Of course, only Septern knew how to make the sun and rain sentient, so to speak.

'What . . . what will this spell do?' asked Sandor, voice tremulous. Janeth caught his eye and saw his own excitement reflected there.

'It will take the light from the sky and the air from every living thing,' said Septern. 'Its components suggest as much, do they not?'

Sandor nodded. 'Over what sort of area do you envisage this spell?'

18

Septern laughed. 'Sandor, are we not here to research the ultimate such that you may learn the whole?

'This spell is the stealer of light. It will create perpetual dark and perfect vacuum. I will call the spell Dawnthief and it will cover *everywhere*.'

## Chapter 2

JANETH HAD WANDERED the grounds for much of the following day after Septern's extraordinary announcement. He felt vaguely disappointed despite the euphoria of the event he had been a party to. Every mage since the dawn of magic had dreamed of developing the ultimate spell. The one that could end everything. All life. And not with the desire for it to be used but to prove that any magic was possible. After all, once the ultimate was proven, all else was simply waiting to be drawn down. Nothing would be beyond the bounds of magic.

And while Janeth had been as carried away as any of them to have witnessed the historical event, he couldn't shake the disappointment. He wasn't unusual, he thought. He just wanted it to have been him. Odd really, because he was here only to witness and use that exact event. Still, every man had his hopes and desires.

Within that disappointment was resentment. Not because he was jealous of Septern's genius: that was a given he admired. No, genius was fine. But why did he have to be such an arrogant bastard with it? Janeth felt that *he* would have handled the whole announcement with a good deal more subtlety and decorum.

He shouldn't have been surprised, then that in the middle of the afternoon, he'd wandered into the stables to see Septern's horse saddled and ready. Shouldn't have been but was. Because riding for the colleges, as he assumed Septern intended, was not merely arrogance: it was suicide.

And there was no way Janeth could allow Septern to die this way, particularly as there was so much to know and so little time to get to know it. So, he determined to take his future in his hands and stop Septern from getting himself killed.

He very nearly succeeded.

Janeth found Septern in the drawing room, searching a bookshelf and whistling to himself. He was dressed for the road in leather in-thighed wool trousers, stout knee length boots and a long, heavy riding cloak. As he turned at Janeth's clearing of his throat, the student could see both white shirt and black undervest.

'Come to wish me safe journey?' he said, his eyes glittering, face shining with energy.

'Nothing could be further from my thoughts,' said Janeth, watching Septern's smile fade. 'There's only one horse saddled at the stables.'

'I always travel alone,' said Septern. 'You know that. I'm not under threat.'

Janeth gaped. The conceit of the man was unbelievable.

'I beg very strongly to differ, Master Septern.'

Septern smiled. 'Worried about the war are you?'

'Aren't you?'

'Not at all. I'm travelling direct to Triverne Lake by the hunter trails. A four-college delegation will meet me there. You don't think for a moment I'd risk myself do you?'

Septern's words, like balm on a wound any other time, merely stoked Janeth's ire.

'Master Septern, I must be allowed to speak freely,' he said, aware he was jittery.

Septern waved a hand impatiently. 'Then be quick about it. Glory awaits me. *Us.*'

'And that is what worries me most,' said Janeth. 'You are, without doubt, the finest living mind in Balaia. And that blinds you to reality. To the Wesmen attacking throughout the east you are not just another mage to be killed. You are their biggest prize. They won't dare attack you here but beyond these grounds? And the Wytch Lords who use them as muscle . . . well, I don't have to tell you the danger they represent to you personally. They know of the threat you pose simply because of the potential of your mind. Should you step outside what guards you, I dread to think of the consequences. Please Master Septern, don't travel. The world has too much more to learn from you. Announcing Dawnthief as you intend is foolhardy. Everyone will want it. Nowhere will be safe. Not even here.'

Septern stood tall, smiling. He walked away from the bookshelf and towards Janeth, placing a hand on the student's shoulder.

'You are my most talented student by a long distance. But you have to understand the nature of my creations. This is research. It is not a spell that will ever be used.'

'Master you don't understand,' Janeth felt panicked by Septern's naivety. 'This is war. Allies and enemies will *demand* Dawnthief for themselves, don't you see?'

'Magic does not stop for conflict,' snapped Septern. His face softened immediately. 'Let me show you something. Stand there and don't move.'

Puzzled but intrigued, Janeth watched Septern stride over to the drawing room doors, close and lock them. He uttered a short incantation and shivered his fingers down the timbers. Mana flowed and fizzed. WardLock. Janeth's heart missed a beat. No one was getting in.

Septern reached into his shirt and pulled out a palm-sized carved amulet. He closed his eyes as he moved back to the centre of the room, mouth moving soundlessly, the amulet clutched tight in his hand. Janeth heard a muffled thud as of shifting air and a depression appeared beneath a rug that covered much of the stone floor.

Opening his eyes, Septern tucked the amulet back inside his shirt and folded the rug aside. There was a hole in the floor. He gestured to it.

'It's not a wine cellar,' he said. 'It's the gateway to wonder. Want to see?'

Janeth nodded mutely, his pulse beating hard in his neck. He knew he was trembling and tried to suppress it. There had long been rumours that Septern had another workshop hidden somewhere in the house. Every student that returned to Dordover had searched. But none had ever found it and Janeth could see why. They had all studied the house plans in the library. There was no cellar beneath the drawing room.

Septern muttered briefly and a LightGlobe the size of his head appeared by his shoulder. He went forwards down a ladder and the light banished the gloom below.

'Come on down,' he called, voice echoing faintly.

Janeth shook himself and walked to the opening, peering down in to what looked like a chill and dusty room. Quite large but apparently unremarkable and with a distinct smell of mustiness about it. He turned and climbed down the ladder to discover how wrong he was.

Occupying much of the wall opposite the ladder was a moving dark panel. Swirls of deep grey with multi-coloured flecks and striated with white poured over each other, endlessly shifting. It roiled and swam within its frame, unnerving and intimidating.

'The world is bigger than you can possibly conceive,' said Septern, all arrogance gone, his tone soft and reverent as he indicated the rip panel. 'But we must take much care over what we find and what we do. Beyond that gate is the reason why. I'll take you there on my return.'

Janeth frowned. 'So why are you showing this to me now? What are you worried might happen?'

'Worried? No, good student.' The high tone was back. 'This is to show you how I and my secrets are truly untouchable. In here lie the secrets to Dawnthief I will not reveal. And through that gate are the keepers of those secrets. Through there I am friend to dragons.' Janeth's jaw must have dropped yet again. 'Believe it Janeth. And so shall you be.'

Janeth studied the rip, his throat dry. He didn't know what to think. This was beyond any dream of what he had hoped he might find. Dragons! All so much myth and children's scare stories. But equally, he had no doubt Septern spoke the truth. He knew the Master's own personal research was focused on the study of alternate dimensions. They were there – Xetesk's cursed alliance with the demons was evidence enough – it was a question of where to find them and what they contained. It seemed Septern had already uncovered some of the answers and all the more reason he didn't undertake his fool's journey.

'Master Septern,' said Janeth, turning from the rip. 'I am truly honoured by your faith in me and I'm looking forward already to working with you in future years. But will I get the chance?'

Septern regarded him silently. He continued.

'Or will these secrets die with you somewhere between here and Triverne Lake? Lost forever in a dimensional workshop no one else can ever touch.'

For the first time, Janeth saw doubt in Septern's eyes. He made the final gamble.

'Unless you leave me knowledge of the way in here, you risk leaving the world nothing but . . . but words and theories. Septern will be a name linked to what *might* have been. Not what *was*.'

Septern felt the amulet through his shirt. 'There is another of these but it's very safe.' He nodded his head at the rip. 'And I swore I would never leave myself without the tools to enter here immediately.' He studied the ground at his feet.

'Master Septern, I'm not saying you *will* die on the road to Triverne, I just believe it's a risk not worth taking. Think what it is you will be offering any that hear you. The owner holds all the cards. Please, if you must deliver Dawnthief, we'll support you in linked Communion with the Dordovan Quorum. Let them use the knowledge wisely and maintain secrecy.'

Septern nodded. 'I hear you Janeth, I really do. But it is a question of *whether* to make the announcement, not *how*. I will not give the world Dawnthief lying on my back in Communion. There is no glory in that.'

'Then delay. Let us work with you to smooth the edges, write the paper and detail the casting. This isn't a spell for growing healthy crops. It's the spell of ultimate destruction . . . and there's a war going on. They will fight over Dawnthief – who *you* are will not matter.'

Septern chewed a lip then gestured Janeth precede him back up the ladder.

'I'll give you my answer in the morning,' he said. 'Have Sandor unsaddle and brush down my horse, would you?'

Janeth smiled. 'Thank you Master Septern. Thank you.'

But in the morning, of course, Septern was gone.

ℋ

Janeth found a note under his door and read it sitting on his bed, his heart sinking, anger building.

*My dear students,*

*Dawnthief cannot be kept from the world. It is too important to the future of magic to allow mere war to stop research. The lore is written though not as straightforward as it could be. Suffice to say that I have made the spell very, very difficult to cast.*

*I will return in fourteen days and we will all celebrate. While I am gone, continue research on the stability of the mana cylinder. By the way, you'll discover an interesting and amusing effect if you introduce a sphere into the crown of the manashape.*

*Don't worry about me. I am untouchable.*

*Septern.*

Dressing hurriedly, Janeth called the others from their rooms to speak over breakfast, each one having read the scribbled note.

'Anyone else feel like I do?' he asked of them.

Sandor nodded and rubbed his hands through his hair.

Dirrion frowned. 'And how do you feel?'

'Like there's trouble coming,' said Janeth.

Dirrion laughed a little nervously. 'He's only going to be away fourteen days. How much trouble can there be?'

'Gods' sake think!' snapped Thuneron. 'He doesn't mean while Septern's gone, he means when he gets back.'

'Why- ?' Dirrion hadn't grasped it. Janeth hushed Thuneron's next outburst.

'Because,' he said quietly. 'Septern is out of touch with the war. He sees himself as separate to it. He doesn't even see the significance of Dawnthief to both sides. He has no real concept of support for the Wytch Lords, within Xetesk in particular. He thinks he's going to deliver Balaia's most important piece of magical research ever. What he's *actually* doing is announcing to any that can hear that he has ownership of the spell that will guarantee victory and eternal dominance.

'Tell me, Dirrion, what would you do to get your hands on the ultimate threat deterrent?'

Dirrion's face had been paling as Janeth spoke. Indeed now he had spelt it out, no one was looking comfortable.

'They'll all be coming here, won't they?' said the small freckled youth.

'*I* would,' said Sandor.

'So I suppose it depends who on gets here first, the colleges or the Wytch Lords,' said Dirrion.

'No, Dirrion,' said Thuneron, dropping a piece of bread back onto this plate. 'You still aren't thinking. Once he's given them the spell, they won't need him anymore. Just the lore and casting papers.'

'You're suggesting a *college* would kill Septern to get Dawnthief?' Dirrion took them all in with his frightened stare.

Sandor's big face was bleak. 'He's saying that power of that magnitude changes everything. And Septern has very few friends anywhere but Dordover these days.'

'But the lore will be Dordovan. No other college will be able to cast it.'

'Will it?' challenged Janeth. 'You've seen Septern's note. And you know what he's capable of. Wouldn't surprise me at all to find it couched in multiple lores just to stop one college getting the upper hand.'

'Remember he doesn't want it cast,' said Sandor. 'To him it's theory and proof of the mastery of magic over the other elements; and that's all.'

'But that won't stop all of them wanting ownership. Because ownership means power, simply because of Dawnthief's potential,' added Thuneron.

'So why is he going there to tell them?' Dirrion's voice was approaching a whine.

'Gods, Dirrion, you may have the mind of a master but you've no grasp of the real world of people!' Thuneron shook his head.

'Look,' said Janeth carefully. 'Septern truly believes himself above conflicts like the war – never mind it's on his doorstep and sweeping across Balaia right now. He only cares about two things when push comes to shove. Developing new magic and then making sure he basks in the glory first hand. I guarantee you he won't have even begun to consider the consequences.'

Another silence followed, contemplative and nervous. Janeth could see them all weighing up their alternatives. So far as he could see, there was only one.

'Well we have to get out of here,' said Dirrion.

Sandor clattered his cup. 'And go where?' he rasped. 'Run if you want, little coward but it won't help you. Are you *genuinely* stupid and blind or have you been working at it?'

Janeth held out a hand to calm the farmer's son. 'Enough, Sandor.'

Sandor's eyes, though, were blazing. 'No, Jan, it's not. We have known exactly what Master Septern's actions will mean from the start. Why couldn't you, Dirrion? And why do you want to run?'

Janeth had to concede Sandor's point. Even Dirrion, who spent every waking hour buried in lore scripts, should have seen this.

'In your own time,' muttered Sandor.

Dirrion wasn't looking at any of them. He hadn't even glanced at Janeth for help.

'Because staying here is death,' he said simply. Now he stared at Sandor. 'Satisfied now? I'm scared. Terrified of what is coming here. And if you aren't, you're as big a fool as you are ugly.'

To Janeth's surprise, Sandor laughed.

'But not scared of me, eh little man?' he said. 'Gods burning, Dirrion, but I can't fathom you. Look, we're *all* scared, I'm sure, but where else can we really go?'

'I don't follow you,' said Dirrion.

'Just for a change,' said Thuneron and they were all laughing, the tension easing.

'Seriously,' said Dirrion eventually.

'I know- ' Thuneron coughed out a mouthful of tea. 'Sorry. What a mess.'

'Look,' said Janeth, determined to bring them back to order. 'It's quite simple. If we run, what happens? Either a college or the Wytch Lords gain Dawnthief and then nowhere is safe. And for those on the loose with knowledge? Well, I'll let you draw your own conclusions but I think "surplus to requirements" about covers it.

'If we stay here, though, we might be able to make a difference.'

Dirrion shook his head. 'You're telling me we four plus Septern can hold off four colleges plus a Wytch Lord-backed Wesmen army?'

'No he's not,' said Sandor. 'All we have to do is hold off whoever gets here first and wait for the rest to show up. That should be a battle to watch.'

'And we can do *that*.' Janeth leant forwards, pushing his plate away. 'Look, I've been thinking.'

## Chapter 3

BALAIA WASN'T AS Septern remembered it. But then he hadn't been outside the extraordinary protection of his grounds for almost two years. Not since he had ridden back with his last set of students. Janeth and his friends had been sent to him as best prospects half a year ago. Ten of them in all. Four was all he ever saw reason to train.

The war had ebbed and flowed across Balaia for a year now, mainly concentrated on the mage lands to the immediate north and east of Understone Pass and the Blackthorne Mountains. But increasingly the Wesmen were moving further south and east. It was a change of tactic to target supply rather than the colleges themselves. But there had never been any doubting the Wytch Lords' principal target.

These six mages of an otherwise shunned form of magic had been expelled from the colleges and eastern Balaia, left to wither and die. But instead, they had prospered. And now, with the considerable might of the Wesmen tribes, they wanted to exact their revenge. Yes, they wanted dominion over Balaia. First, though, they wanted to reduce modern magic to dust and scorched earth.

In truth, much of the year had been little more than a stand-off. Following the first surprising and damaging incursions into the east, the Wesmen and their masters had been halted by a combination of allied magic and a call to arms from the Barons and Lords of the powerful Korina Trade Alliance.

But it had left Balaia a suspicious land. Communities across the continent locked their doors to strangers, fearing the merciless Wesmen raiding parties that burned, murdered and stole to feed their armies. Any that could, hired mercenaries. Those that couldn't, begged their local lord or the colleges for protection. Burned timbers and rotting corpses told of those whose pleas were ignored.

Septern steered clear of towns and villages, choosing to take the hunters' paths he had always travelled to the colleges. Hidden in forest, or small and lost against shale, crag or summer-dried grassland, he looked at the dying country with a detached sadness.

He hadn't been part of Balaia's society for two decades but he bore it no ill will. And, he reflected, he still needed Balaia, or who would be there to hear his words or to bring meat and grain to feed him? The Wesmen hated magic, only bending the knee to the Wytch Lords through fear and some fluke of religious mistaken identity.

Septern, whose roots in magic were far more akin to the Wytch Lords than any college, despised them for their perversion of magic. They could not see its glory, only its capacity for destruction and dominion. And he, Septern, would never reveal anything of worth to them.

He needed Balaia and its people but they were too scared to show themselves. Crops went untended, livestock roamed unchecked. He was six days travelling to Triverne and every isolated farmstead he passed was deserted. Small hamlets had been fired and abandoned to stop the Wesmen using them. Towns were stockaded and defended. Muscle was pre-eminent alongside the scent of fear.

But there was no sound of life. All was still. In the forest, the animals felt it. On the plains, the livestock bunched silent where they roamed. In the towns, they feared a shout could bring down the hordes of the Wesmen. Or worse, the Wytch Lords.

The last night before he arrived at Triverne Lake, Septern camped in a cleft between two steep crags. He tethered his horse by a quick running stream and lay back, shunning fire and food, to think.

There was something in what Janeth had said. The lad was bright, no doubt about that, and Septern had to concede the war had altered Balaia far more than he had envisaged.

But Dawnthief itself wasn't the answer and even Janeth had missed that. The spell was theory only. Yes, Septern had written the lore and had with him a draft casting paper but even so . . . The mana shape testing had not even been started, the stability matrix wasn't plotted and the expansion rate graph had not been drawn. And that was on the most basic level. Gods, nothing had been certified other than the, theoretical notion that the spell could be cast. And although Septern was supremely confident his calculations were right, even he wouldn't attempt a casting yet.

He smiled to himself as he settled back to watch the stunted trees immediately above him move in the warm summer night breeze. Anyhow, he thought, anyone casting from the notes he would make public at Triverne Lake wouldn't get very far. The lore he had not disclosed to anyone saw to that. It contained three catalysts and he defied anyone to bring them together in one place, even should they discover their identity.

Once lore was bound to the manashape, it could not be undone and Septern had already conducted the binding rituals in his workshop.

No, Dawnthief was not a spell that would ever be cast. It would remain as he designed it, a key to unlock every other secret magic still kept.

And with it, his name would forever be inscribed in the annals of history.

)(

It took the students three days to source and map all the wards, alarms, illusions and booby traps surrounding Septern's grounds. Janeth feared it would take longer but Dirrion remembered a plan he'd unrolled weeks before, thinking it was a lore scroll. It listed every static spell covering the Manse itself.

But still, the task was daunting. Septern's grounds – which included orchards, a lake, lawns, stables, barns, a paddock, fallow fields and a series of empty tenant cottages – covered in excess of thirty five acres. Theoretically, they should have simply been able to plot a mana map by probing with their minds from the comfort of their beds. But nothing regarding Septern's arrangements was ever as it seemed.

The illusions were simple enough. Not just because the constructs were so robust and therefore obvious, but because their effects were there to see the moment you stepped outside them.

Janeth had to concede they were impressive. Flawless, actually. One pace, he'd been looking out from Septern's lands towards the Pontois Plains, the next he could look back to discover that the house and buildings had been replaced by impenetrable forest or, from the south, by sheer cliff.

It was the same from above, too. Dirrion had over-flown the grounds to find the dozen illusions flowing seamlessly to create a landscape of woodland, crag and plateau. Beautiful but empty.

But the extraordinary illusions were not the real reason Septern was so dismissive of the threat of war, despite his isolation and not employing a single swordsman for his defence. After all, anyone could stumble through an illusion.

At the heart of his unshakable confidence were the multiple rings of wards, most of which were invisible even to a searching mage. Triggered by complex equations covering recognition of certain classes of movement across its map, any ward could activate on sensing threat and, in so doing, link to the connecting net of surrounding spells.

There was an intricate linkage in the shapes and, presumably, the lore structures of each ward that connected them to one another. For, while all the constructs were recognisable, every single one had been altered.

'I don't know how he does it,' said Dirrion, poring over the grid they had drawn.

'I think that's the idea,' said Sandor.

'I mean, he could stop an army with this lot.'

'I think that's the idea,' the three chorused.

'Very funny,' said Dirrion into the laughter.

The four students were sitting in armchairs pulled up to the edges of the centre of the drawing room. The rug had been rolled to one side and the grid had been sketched in chalk on the stone-flagged floor; a spread of books at its centre indicated the house and larger outbuildings. It was early evening and the days of research had left them all shattered.

'Sorry, Dirry,' said Janeth. 'You were going to explain something.'

Dirrion nodded. 'Yes. We've had to follow the merest hints in the mana trails to find even the outer circle of wards. The rest of the rings we've inferred by linkage only and the overall drain from the wards as a whole, traced backwards to source. The first thing I don't understand is how all of these wards can possibly have hidden mana constructs, though they plainly do. The second is, there are over nine hundred separate wards guarding the grounds and two hundred more covering the house. Even given the stability of their constructs, the residual drain has to be huge. There's no way even Septern can feed in that amount of mana regularly enough to maintain them – not without us noticing it.

'So where in all the hells is it coming from?'

A puffing of cheeks, a shaking of heads, a shrug of shoulders.

'He must be drawing it from the chaos stream,' said Thuneron eventually.

'We'd have seen that,' said Dirrion. 'And so would anyone looking into the mana spectrum.'

'They could be self-sustaining,' said Sandor, his hand describing a disc. 'You know, like a circuit, each one draining into the next.'

'I think up to a point they are,' said Dirrion. 'But there's still overall drain that we've seen weaken parts of the grid.'

'I'm surprised he'd allow even that imperfection,' said Thuneron.

'He wouldn't,' said Janeth. 'Unless there was a compelling reason why he should.'

That stopped them. Janeth watched brows furrow as the quartet searched for an answer.

'So what are we left with?' asked Sandor.

'Wards that drain but shouldn't and a reservoir of mana that feeds them. Only we can't see it or use it even though we know it has to be there,' said Janeth.

'Is this relevant?' asked Thuneron. 'The fact is, we've got a big work load and not that much time.'

'Yes, it's relevant,' replied Dirrion. 'Because Septern's powering all this from somewhere and if we can find out where, we can have all these spells fully functional in no time.'

Janeth nodded and gazed back across the grid, its multi-coloured lines tracing the links as far as they could determine.

Even with the four of them working each day until their stamina was exhausted, they wouldn't be able to maintain all of the eleven hundred static spells before Septern returned. In fact, they would be lucky to get through a third.

'What's your estimate of the overall state of the grid?' he asked Dirrion.

From apperaing as part pariah, the freckled lore genius had assumed the mantle of central figure.

'Oh, it's not at all bad right now,' said Dirrion. 'But the drain is significant and I think there's a certain exponentiality to it. If we don't do anything, I'd expect at least three quarters of the wards to be inoperative or, at best, not at optimum operation.'

There was a hiss of indrawn breath around the room. Janeth raised his eyebrows and looked over at Sandor. The big farmer's son wore a deep frown.

'Why would he leave us so undefended?' asked Thuneron in a voice that hinted at betrayal.

'He doesn't think he has,' replied Janeth. 'He's so sure no one will attack here he didn't even consider telling us about the extent or state of the grid.'

'Either that or he was so full of thoughts of glory that he forgot,' said Sandor in a low voice.

Janeth shook his head. 'I doubt that. I just think he knows he can ride back in here and uncork the mana, so to speak.' He paused to draw breath. 'Thing is, we can't risk that not happening. After all, he may never come back. Can I make a suggestion?'

Gestures and nods bade him carry on.

'There's got to be lore script somewhere and a casting paper that covers the method Septern uses for charging all these static spells. I suggest Dirrion carries on looking while we three begin the maintenance first thing tomorrow. Dirrion can you advise us where to start?'

Dirrion nodded. 'I'll mark up the grid. There are zones of relative strength and weakness. I'd suggest beginning with the outer circle. If there's any flaw in Septern's grid it's that the first words have to trip the second circle or parts of the whole won't activate.'

Janeth nodded and glanced at the other two.

'Happy with that?'

'It's the best plan we've got,' said Thuneron.

'It's the *only* plan we've got,' said Sandor with a smile, and when his eyes met Janeth's, they held a satisfied gleam.

⩎

Septern rested his arms on the lectern and drank in a heartbeat's glorious silence. The lecture had gone exactly as he had planned on his journey. Building the promise and then pulling the rug – inviting debate and question. Now all that remained was to see which of the fifty bemused senior and master mage faces straightened enough to ask him the most obvious question.

In the late morning heat of a blue-skied summer's day, the canvas walls of the ceremonial marquee had been folded away, leaving just the canopy to keep the sun at bay. A gentle breeze blew through the marquee, ruffling the clothes and robes of the four-college delegates sitting on the ranks of chairs before Septern – the only mage for whom they would turn out in these numbers to hear speak.

Behind him, the blue waters of Triverne Lake glittered in the sunlight, sea birds calling as they swooped low. The lush waterside vegetation crammed with colour, swept up the western hillsides, basking. It was the most beautiful and tranquil spot. A pity mages used it to argue death, suspicion and destruction.

The noise started with a murmuring. One turning to another to check they had heard Septern correctly. The voices gained in volume, accusing words flying between the Xeteskian and Dordovan delegations while those of Julatsa and Lystern turned to the speaker himself, demanding he clarify his last statement. Septern watched them, a half smile playing about his lips. He could pretend he didn't understand their expressions for as long as they chose not to address him directly. Eventually, an old Julatsan elf he didn't recall asked the question.

'You understand the gravity of our situation. Ultimately the Wytch Lords will engulf even you as well unless they are stopped. Why will you not give us Dawnthief?' The discontented murmuring stopped. 'And by us I mean all of us. All four colleges.'

Silence but for the rustling of canvas and the call of birds.

Septern could even hear the lake waters lapping gently on the shore. He smiled. His glory was not in mere adulation. It was in knowing that they did not really understand . . . that for all their power, they were lesser mages than him.

'Because you don't need it. Not the complete spell.' He paused. 'You have no vision, any of you. Clearly only I can see the potential of my discovery applied to other more, shall we say, gentle spells.' He watched them all frown at once, fragile egos pricked.

'Dawnthief is not a spell designed to be cast, which is why I will be leaving you with incomplete information. It is a spell to open your eyes. Do you really not have the wit to study its shape and apply it to castings that can be used against the Wytch Lords?'

He shook his head. 'You are among the finest mage minds in Balaia. Please don't make me doubt you.'

'Our need is now,' snapped the Dordovan High Master, Arteche, his gravelled voice echoing out. 'Dawnthief will win us this war quickly and minimise bloodshed on both sides. Its deterrent alone will force our enemies back beyond the Blackthorne Mountains. We don't need to use the spell, but we do have to own it.'

'I sympathise, my Lord Arteche, I really do. But deterrent is nothing without demonstration, is it? How would you convince our esteemed enemies of your veracity otherwise? What I have given you allows you to fine tune every spell in your Book and stabilise the cage you are developing to entrap the Wytch Lords. Dawnthief will win you the war, but not by being used as a threat.

'Put your best researchers and analysts on the text. I must return home where I can be of more use to you. I believe that concludes this lecture.'

No one clapped. He had not expected them to though some small token of gratitude wouldn't have gone amiss. Perhaps when the war was over and won because of this day, they would stop to think. A pity their greed and base desires closed their minds to what he had really given them. Balaia's magic was run by fools.

The noise of angry voices grew, joined by the scraping of chairs. At least they knew better than to keep questioning him once he'd closed the lecture. That was the way. In the end, they would see he was right. Septern hoped it happened before too many more men died but there was a principle at stake here and he would not compromise it, not even to end a war. It was too dangerous.

In the emptying auditorium, Bynaar, one of the Xeteskian Circle Seven, remained in close and animated conversation with the Dordovan, Helothe. The two middle-aged men were not seeing eye to eye. No surprise there. As Septern watched, Bynaar turned his head and their eyes met. The Xeteskian's scowl could have peeled paint. He glowered from under heavy brows and shook his head slowly and deliberately. Septern smiled back. Though an impressive mage, Bynaar held no fear for him. Not him nor his bickering Circle.

Septern began gathering his papers, separating his speech notes from the bundle he would leave with Arteche. His old tutor could at least be relied upon to see the work copied and given to each college. Below him, soldiers from the four-college guard began stacking chairs onto covered carts and already, beyond the fringes of the marquee, some of the mages were mounted and leaving, shadowed by bodyguards.

Below the lectern, a soldier cleared his throat.

'Excuse me, sir, but we need to stow the marquee. Might I ask you to move outside?'

'Yes, of course,' said Septern.

He tied a ribbon round the research papers and walked out into the sudden glare of the sun, shading his eyes with a hand. Arteche was waiting by his horse, his guards nearby and the rest of the Dordovan delegation gathered to his left. Septern walked over and handed him the papers,

'It makes good reading,' he said lightly.

Arteche scowled, the ageing master staring along his long narrow nose.

'I am sure it does,' he said, stowing the bundle in a saddle bag. 'You put me and the whole college in a very difficult position.'

'How so? Presumably you'll share all these papers. No one gets more or less. All the tools are there to win this war.'

'That isn't what I mean as you well know. Walk with me a while.'

'Master Arteche, you know I never speak with individuals

after a lecture. It only leads to more and more questions ... people get jealous.'

Arteche grabbed Septern's arm above the elbow with a surprisingly strong grip, bony fingers digging into his flesh.

'For once in your life, listen,' Arteche said, his voice a rasping whisper. 'What you have done here today is folly beyond anything else your ridiculous ego has ever lulled you into.' The grip hardened. 'Walk with me.'

Septern nodded mutely, stung by Arteche's words. He flashed back to his student days under the same master, for whom he had enormous respect, and reflected that age had not changed his manner.

Walking past knots of mages and soldiers, Septern saw repeated glances and frowns as members of every delegation tried to gauge what they were seeing. You could almost smell the suspicion.

At the lakeside, crunching across a narrow stretch of sand and small pebbles, Arteche released his grip.

'You wanted to tell me something?' Septern said, attempting to sound off-hand but not succeeding. He felt small again, out of control. It was not a situation with which he was comfortable.

'Have you learned nothing of the nature of man? Of mage man in particular?' Arteche's pleasant tone held a simmering intent.

'Have - ?'

'Has your exile in your grand mansion and grounds really divorced you so well from actuality that your eyes cannot see what would be obvious to a crawling infant?'

Arteche's words flew like splinters. Septern shrugged.

'I'm sorry, I – '

'Don't apologise to me, Septern. It's your genius you are wasting. It's your death warrant you have just signed. We have your papers. We know you have completed the spell's lore. There must be a record. What need have we of you?'

For the first time he could readily recall, Septern felt confused. Hurt.

'You will always need me,' he said, his words ringing tonelessly in his head.

'And do you think all those who come after you will think that far? You'll be needing all your apparently clever defence simply to stay alive, but it still won't be enough.'

Septern frowned. 'I don't understand. I've given you the answers.'

'But not the prize!' snapped Arteche, clenching a fist. 'And men will do anything to get hold of it.'

Quite suddenly, all the anger was gone from his voice, his body. He put an arm round Septern's shoulders and leant in, both men looking more over the placid surface of the lake than at each other.

'Dordover can offer you genuine security,' said the old master. 'We can defend you against anything our enemies throw against us. Yes it will set us against our fledgling allies too but when all is said and done, you are a son of Dordover. It is out duty to protect you.'

'Our enemies,' repeated Septern, his heart thumping uncomfortably, his mind one pace adrift.

'The Wytch Lords, Xetesk. Julatsa even.'

'Your enemies, not mine.'

'And all will kill you to get Dawnthief for themselves.'

'But without me, no one will ever understand it.'

'Do you really think that will occur to them or even that they will believe it? Septern, please. Think what you have unleashed. You are bringing war to your doorstep.'

'But the Wytch Lords weren't here to listen,' said Septern, hearing echoes of Janeth in every word Arteche spoke.

'No?' Arteche turned from the lake and let his gaze rove over the clearing filled with mages and soldiers. 'You think they don't have ears even here? And whether what they will hear scares them or not, doesn't matter. Because they will not run west, will they? Whoever owns Dawnthief, owns the world.'

## Chapter 4

ARTECHE HAD LEFT him alone to think while he found a man to prepare Septern's horse. But now he was coming back. In the intervening time, Septern had found himself trembling, unable to look back at the mages he had thought were in awe of him but who he now was supposed to believe would kill him for what he hid.

Preposterous. Yet Arteche had never been given to fanciful notions. And he did know these people in ways Septern did not. Even so, Septern felt the colleges would be looking to save him and his secrets from any invasion by the Wytch Lords as opposed to taking it for themselves. After all, what he had already given them was the gift of the generation. Surely they would settle for it, once they took the time to study his findings.

But again, Arteche appeared so genuine in his offer to protect. But from whom? His riding to Dordover would undoubtedly cause more tension between the colleges at a time they could ill afford it. They had to have unity now or they would be destroyed. And if he went to Dordover, what of Dawnthief? And what of his students? Innocent young men who would have nowhere to run. Janeth had spoken of the risks Septern was taking but he had chosen to ignore them. The youth and Arteche spoke the same language, held the same fears.

There was really only one course of action for Septern to take.

'Your horse is ready, Septern. We need to leave shortly. There's a good distance to travel to the first secure camp,' Arteche said as he strode up. 'You are going to do the right thing, I trust?'

40

'Oh yes,' said Septern. 'I am.' He looked Arteche in the eye. 'I've got students at the Manse. If you're right, I can't leave them there to die because of me.'

'Very laudable. Very honourable,' said Arteche. 'We can commune with them. Bring them out before anything happens to them. There is no reason for you to go back there.'

Septern shook his head. 'I promised them I'd be back. I can't leave them, I can't leave Dawnthief.'

'You aren't thinking straight. I know you too well. Face it, Septern, you haven't left any critical information on Dawnthief anywhere anyone could find it.'

'There's always a chance,' said Septern. 'And there's far more to be defended than Dawnthief. It's you who doesn't understand.'

Arteche sighed. 'No I don't. Perhaps you'd like to enlighten me.' The master was agitated, anxious to leave. 'Quickly.'

'I must seal the gateway.'

'Where is it?'

'It doesn't matter to you, Master Arteche. It must be sealed. I have a responsibility. And my students cannot carry it out for me.'

'Gods but you are a difficult man, Septern of Dordover.' Arteche pushed a hand across his thinning hair.

Septern smiled. 'The Manse is not ready to be left.'

'We'll send a guard with you. Secure your passage there and back to Dordover.'

'No, my Lord. Save your men to guard yourself. I will not be coming to Dordover.'

'Septern you cannot hope to defend yourself against an army!' Arteche couldn't help but raise his voice. Out in the shallows, birds took to flight. 'Damn you for a fool – when they find you, they'll kill you and take the prize.'

'"They, they",' said Septern. 'Then keep them from my borders and let me do my work. I do appreciate your offer but I have already said I will be of greater use to you in my own workshop. No Wesman will cross my threshold while I still live. No Wytch Lord shall find my workshop whether I live or die. I shall I see to it. I leave it to the duty of Dordover to keep my enemies from interrupting me.'

Arteche nodded and looked at the ground, speaking his final words as he turned. 'I fear for you, Septern. Look to your defence and do not leave it until too late to run, wherever it is you believe you can run to.'

'Worry about yourselves,' replied Septern. 'Read my research. Commune with me. Defeat the Wytch Lords.'

But as he watched Arteche walk away, he began to wonder whether the colleges were capable.

)(

The firelight in the first secure camp was bright in the midnight sky. Stars were a rash across the heavens. Most of the delegations were asleep in their tents, their soldiers patrolling beyond the perimeters, their bodyguards close by. Arteche sat with the Xeteskian, Byaar, the silence between them reflective and friendly.

'He has always been a stubborn man,' said Byaar eventually.

'To the point of stupidity. And in one so clever, well . . .' Arteche shook his head.

'Do you think he can do what he says?'

Arteche chuckled. 'If he's left alone, I have no doubt he can help us bring about an end to the Wytch Lords.'

'Not going to happen, though, is it?'

'No indeed,' said Arteche. 'But I've done all I can for him. And we are out of time.'

'Yes,' agreed Byaar. 'But we must do at least one thing he asks and keep the Wesmen and Wytch Lords from his door.'

'I think we can all agree to do that,' said Arteche, feeling a sadness for his most gifted of former students.

'So we can.' Byaar's smile was cold. 'So we can.'

)(

With night full and his horse sleeping under the influence of a calming spell, Septern sat awake in the cool air, a blanket around his shoulders and alarm wards defending his camp. He had wanted a fire to keep his spirits up but knew it would attract his enemies.

Enemies. Gods burning but he never thought he'd have to

think like this on the way home from Triverne Lake. But on this first day's ride back, the enormity of what Arteche had said had hit home. Mages would murder their most gifted brother to get hold of a spell that could end the world.

They were blind, all of them. And he had to suspect even Arteche and Dordover, he supposed. Why would they be different? And the attraction of having him – Septern – within their walls was obvious. After all, he could recreate the spell there, couldn't he? He presumed he should count himself lucky that the presence of the four college delegations stopped Dordover from forcing him into their clutches.

He stopped himself there, jumping to his feet and pacing round in a tight circle. Above him, leaves rustled on branches and clouds swept across the star-filled sky. What was he thinking? Would Arteche of all people really betray him? The great master had been his most fervent supporter. The man who encouraged him to leave the college and work in the solitude of the Manse. The man who was one of the few to know of the gateway to the dimensions and to have met the Kaan himself. He had seemed so genuinely concerned yet he had missed the obvious and wanted to ignore it – Dawnthief and the gateway were there and couldn't be left for enemies to find.

Septern could not get away from it; with him not there, it would make things a whole lot easier for anyone who wanted to gain access to the Manse and workshop. Or so they thought. He fingered the amulet on his chest.

He sat back down again, his back to a tree. How had he been so stupid? Yet he really had believed they'd all see it his way. That Dawnthief was the door to the answers and not the answer itself. He should have listened to Janeth. His favourite student had seen it straight away . . . had told him not to travel. Of course they might all be wrong and he might still be right. Perhaps they would read his papers before they acted. One thing was certain, he could rely on the colleges to do all they could to keep the Wytch Lords from gaining the secret.

But it was better to be as safe as he could be. War did strange things to people's minds; as did power just beyond their grasp. Septern felt confused and hurt by events yet almost childishly happy to be travelling back to the Manse for at least one good reason. And considering his students who he would not suffer to be killed over his folly, he settled back to attempt Communion with Janeth. There was much to be done and he was far from home.

$$\text{\char"2653}$$

'It has gone exactly as we feared,' said Janeth over their hasty breakfast. Though he had received the Communion from Septern late the previous night, he had not had the heart to wake them. The maintenance schedule for the wards was exhausting and they were all showing the effects in drawn, dark faces, often unshaven, and sullen broken conversation. The only time they slept was to replenish mana stamina for the next session. 'I've been contacted by Septern.'

All eyes were on him. Aileen, who had been pouring tea, made a polite retreat back to the kitchen. Janeth had already spoken to her and, once Septern arrived back at the Manse, had advised her to leave.

'It's all bad, is it?' asked Sandor, face still relatively unlined. The farmer's son's natural fitness had better prepared him for the punishment their bodies had taken.

'Not entirely. Septern's reason for contact was to get us working on the essential maintenance he feels he might not have time to attend to when he returns. Naturally, the fact we'd already mapped every ward and begun exactly the process he wanted has made him very happy. Not just because we're doing it but because we worked it all out without him.' Janeth watched their faces crack into weary smiles. Praise from the master was rare and to be enjoyed, even second hand and at a time like this.

'Should we all survive, we can tell our children all about it,' said Dirrion. The lore genius had only just started applying his mind to the maintenance itself having completed his library research. He had found no work concerning any kind of mana reservoir for the ward grid.

'Oh, we'll survive,' said Janeth. 'Septern's given me a couple of tips about faster ways to get around the wards. We'll not be so far behind tonight though it won't improve our tiredness.'

'What about the bad news, then?' asked Sandor.

'I expect you can guess. Arteche has as much as told him that every army in Balaia will be descending on this house in the next few days because they all want Dawnthief for themselves not just a few scabby bits of extrapolated research potential.'Janeth shook his head in frustration. 'I did try to warn him.'

'Knowing he wouldn't listen,' said Thuneron.

'I had to try. Anyway, it changes nothing. Just makes things more difficult for us all. Oh, and by the way it means Aileen has to go now. Before things get serious.' Janeth shrugged.

'But what if the wrong people get here first?' Dirrion was wringing his hands.

'Eleven hundred wards says they don't get in here before the relief arrives,' smiled Sandor.

Janeth chuckled. 'This is what we were born for, you know, all of us. To be at the centre of a world-changing event.'

'You think it'll be that, do you?' Thuneron sipped at his tea.

'Absolutely. We're history in the making.'

'Or just history if we don't sort these wards,' said Sandor. 'Time to get back to work.'

'Five days before Septern gets back here. Let's make sure we don't disappoint him.' Janeth pushed back his chair, feeling his legs protest. Amazing really. He was spending the day sitting outside or in, casting spells and directing mana. He had barely exercised a muscle yet he felt as though he had been pushing a plough for a month. It was yet something else non-mages would never understand.

)(

Two days out from the Manse and Septern had cause to send a prayer to the gods that his trails wouldn't suffer an army to travel. Narrow crags and dense forests; hidden vales and tight river valleys. He knew he was being followed but wasn't unduly worried. He had been expecting it for a couple of days now and was almost comforted to be proved right. Agents of whom, he had not the slightest idea. All he did know was that there was a change in the mood of the country.

The sun shone as it had for days, the empty farms and towns still stood idle, cattle died in the fields for want of milking, but there was something on the air, or more accurately, on the mana.

The spectrum buzzed and crackled with spell activity. It appeared as oases of order in the chaos that was mana in its natural state. Normally, when monitoring the mana spectrum, a mage would do well to distinguish any casting from the maelstrom. It was like trying to spot a salmon in a river. All but impossible except at spawning times when the dash upriver meant you couldn't help but see. Mana activity was like that right now.

It would be Communion to a large extent as the colleges marshalled forces. They served as a sign to extinguish Septern's vain hope that Arteche was wrong. The colleges were on the move, none willing to reach their goal later than the others. Battle was inevitable. Where that battle would be joined was less easy to determine.

Already, great spikes in the spectrum spoke of a host of offensive and defensive spells deployed in a hurry, no doubt in some clash probably in the mage lands. Septern sighed as he returned his vision to a normal state. The fools would destroy each other and do the Wytch Lords' job for them. All for a spell.

For the first time, Septern regretted having made the discovery.

But that wasn't something he could wallow in now. Because while the mage spies were across the land sending back reports of troop movements to their commanders, there was something out there that he sincerely hoped was taxing the brightest tactical brains in every college city. Wesmen. Tens of thousands of Wesmen. Pouring across the northern approaches of Thornewood, they came. Breaking off from conflicts at Xetesk and Blackthorne, ignoring the mage lands that were their main focus and running east. Running to the Manse.

He could see them from where he sat, his sight augmented to disperse the dusk. A seething mass, their standards flying, their lords mounted and riding beside the columns, exhorting them to greater effort. Single-minded, determined, ruthless. It was in the way they ran, the set of their bodies and the energy of their songs. Small wonder they believed they could sweep all of Balaia and its magic before them. And behind them, the trail of their destruction mapped out in the columns of smoke pouring from a hundred torched farmsteads and homes.

The gods alone knew how many of them there were exactly

but Septern could see only one saving grace. When he probed the mana spectrum around them, there was no dark morass, no diseased order emanating out to blight what it touched. No chill. The Wytch Lords were not with them. Presumably, they were still in Parve, disseminating their orders through the Shamen that travelled with the warrior hordes.

Septern shivered. At the pace they travelled, they would reach the vicinity of the Manse before him. How long they took to breach the illusions was anybody's guess. It would depend on the power of the Wytch Lords over such a distance and the willingness of the Wesmen to disbelieve what was apparently in front of them. It would buy him some time and he whispered thanks to the foresight of his students whose assessment of his ward grid would have ensured that the illusions, alarms and first series of traps at the borders of his lands were at peak capacity.

Again, there was only one course of action open to Septern. He could have attempted to ride around and ahead of the Wesmen but that way was fraught and he risked their scouts seeing him disappear into the illusions. No. Much as he cared for his horse, it was time the mare took her own chances.

Despite the dramatic reduction in available mana stamina available to him when he arrived at the Manse a day before the Wesmen, Septern would have to deploy ShadowWings and fly the remaining distance under the cover of darkness.

Septern turned from the scene below him to look over at his horse, standing calmly grazing at a low leafy shrub. He walked towards her, smiling. A twig snapped to his left. Septern stopped, facing the sound. He heard a low gasp and a dull thud.

'Oh dear,' he whispered. 'Carelessly close, I think.'

Curiosity, as always, got the better of him and he picked his way quietly towards the source of the sound. He could see the shape of a body about fifty yards away.

Moving to the corpse, he knelt down and pulled it face up. The woman's expression was of surprise, her blue-tinged lips slightly apart, a line of drool hanging from the corner of her mouth.

The ward she had tripped had sent a targeted mana coil straight into her chest. With the speed of a striking snake, it had enveloped her heart and squeezed. She had never stood a chance.

Septern frowned and probed the mana flowing across her. He stiffened. She was not a mage . . . and yet they had sent her to track Balaia's best ever.

'Fools,' he said. The ward had a signature even a novice could detect. It was its own warning to come no closer. But you had to be a mage to know danger lurked ahead. He did not mean for the ward to activate and kill. But then he hadn't expected to be followed by non mages.

He wondered briefly which college had sent her and realised that was why she was not a mage. If she died, they didn't want him to know.

'Oh, Arteche, what have you done? What have I done?'

There would be more, Septern was certain of that. He was equally certain they wouldn't find him. He waited for full dark, took bit, bridle and saddle from his horse and set her free to roam while he took to the skies, saddle bags across one shoulder, ShadowWings trimmed for speed, and raced for the Manse.

# Chapter 5

SEPTERN HAD FLOWN high and fast, passing directly over the Wesmen as they camped. He could see their fires far below, golden yellow pools on the black landscape, shadows flicking around their extremities. Once or twice, he fancied he caught snatches of conversation but knew it had to be the wind playing tricks as it rushed past his ears.

It was an eerie sensation and he felt unsafe despite his position. There was no way a Wesman could possibly have sensed him, let alone see him. But he concentrated hard nonetheless, the ShadowWings powering him on, occasionally glancing back over his shoulder and berating himself for his idiocy every time.

Well past the vanguard of the horde, Septern reached the vicinity of the Manse an hour before dawn. Coming in from the north, he was presented with dark, impenetrable evergreen forest rising up the slopes of a range of hills.

Septern flew on towards the spectacular night-shrouded illusion, Wings whispering on the air, only to pull up and away at the last instant. Wesmen scouts were no further than a mile from the illusion's edge.

He caught only a glimpse. But it was enough to know they were three in number and confused. One had been pointing, one scowling and the third looking at a parchment in his hands. As Septern rose, his heart thudded wildly, waiting for the shouts. They never came and he exhaled the breath he had been unconsciously holding.

For a few beats he hovered, irritated. His plan had been to land immediately inside the illusory boundary and walk in, checking the state of the northern ward grid. He had wanted to walk through the door with the assessment on his lips; assume control in an instant.

That was now out of the question and he had to assume similar groups of scouts were slowly closing in on all fronts. He only hoped they were all as puzzled by the absence of a mansion house.

He smiled briefly but quashed it. The situation was more dangerous that he had suspected and he wondered, not for the first time, how it was they had managed to get the drop in the colleges so comprehensively.

It was almost as though they had known the content of his lecture even before he'd given it.

Dismissing the thought, he rose higher, meaning to arrow in directly over the Manse at the centre of the ward field. It was still full dark. There shouldn't be a problem.

)(

Janeth crawled towards consciousness from a sleep induced by a ninth successive stamina-draining day. None of them had any real concept of the effects constant spell casting wrought – even simple mana flow castings such as they had been undertaking.

He felt an exhaustion that slowed his every thought and movement, periodically blurred his eyesight and affected his hearing and appetite. His arms had weights hanging from them, his legs waded through thick mud and his rib cage protested every breath.

He had seen the signs in the others too. And all their tempers were short and ragged. More than once, they had all but come to blows. Ultimately though, their task had drawn them away from the brink. And though they had to concentrate on casting the spells, still the number of unmaintained wards fell. Janeth expected Septern to be impressed. He expected it to be enough to earn the trust and respect they deserved. That was vital.

What he hadn't expected to see was Septern framed in his bedroom doorway. At least it answered the question of why he had woken up.

'I apologise for disturbing you,' said Septern quietly, moving towards him.

Janeth's mind, still befuddled by sleep and surprise, thwarted his attempts to phrase a coherent question.

'What.... so why...'

'You're risking your health, all of you. I have an antidote for that.'

Too late Janeth realised Septern was casting. And as the Master's hand touched him lightly on the forehead, he slipped into a deep slumber, his soundless voice protesting all the way.

)(

It was a gamble Septern had to take. Exhausted students with dried wells of mana stamina would be no good to him if he were to succeed.

Dawnthief could bring about the end of the war but not in the way any of the colleges suspected. And strangely, it was good that the Wesmen were here first. They were here in great numbers, presumably to take the spell and fight off any attempt to stop them. But they had seriously miscalculated the similar desire of some or all of the colleges. There would be a battle here that would shape history but only if he, Septern, could make a few things happen.

He had to contact Arteche to ensure enough college forces were committed; he had to hold the Wesmen off until they arrived and he had to secure the critical Dawnthief catalyst information beyond any wit in case the Wesmen broke through.

He felt tired just thinking about it and the fact that his flight and the quartet of the romantically titled DreamShaper spells had put significant strain on his reserves of mana stamina.

What he had to do would take a full day of rest and casting. He was confident that the ward grid would resist a concerted Wesmen attack given their fear of magic . . . and their defencelessness against it – but what state the grid would be in following that attack was his anxiety. With no mages overseeing drain in any particular sectors, there was no ability to transfer mana to weakening spells. If the Wesmen pushed at one area alone, it was conceivable that they could reach, though not breach, the Manse before the students awoke.

Yet their condition had left him with no option. DreamShaper was designed to open mind and body to replenishment of mana and basic physical energy. Without it, none of them would be able to help him for long enough. Not Sandor, with his bull's strength, not Janeth with his incredible casting efficiency and certainly not the other two.

With every moment vital, Septern fetched bread, meat and water from the kitchen and headed to the drawing room. In the insipid glow of pre-dawn light, he paused long enough to be impressed by the accuracy of the chalk rendering of the grid before pulling the amulet from his chest and opening up the dimension door to his workshop.

Sealing the door above him, and scattering the food on his already cluttered desk, Septern lit a pair of lanterns and opened his journal to the last entry. A blank page was opposite and he picked up a quill to write but discarded it just as quickly. There was going to be only one more entry and it could be completed only when his tasks were done. First, Arteche.

Settling back in his chair, Septern closed his eyes and shaped a Communion. His mind reached out across the blazing mana spectrum, the spell searching for the unique spike that represented Arteche. Like seeing a single mountain peak in a shifting range, the spike loomed from the mass, its strength telling Septern that Arteche was close but perhaps not close enough.

The Communion butted against the Master's innate and powerful mind shield, gained through decades of learning and experience. For his part, Arteche recognised the caster of the Communion and granted him immediate access. The two mind voices flowed within the spell.

'I apologise for waking you, Master Arteche,' said Septern.

'I was not asleep,' came the terse reply. 'To what do I owe the pleasure?'

'We can pretend if we like but it will serve no one but the Wytch Lords. I've monitored the spectrum, I've heard your warnings and I know you are closer to me than you are your own chambers. You have come for the spell.'

Septern's heart sank with every word. Like naming the beast, it gave reality to fear.

'Dordover has come to protect you as we said we would. Some of our brother colleges don't have your survival as priority.'

'And you are discussing this with them as you ride, presumably,' said Septern. 'Please don't take me for a bigger fool than I have already been for believing I could trust my fellow mages.'

'Septern, you must believe me - '

'No, Master Arteche,' said Septern quietly. 'There is nothing I *must* do for you. But you will listen to me. The Wytch Lords hunt my signature through the mana and the Wesmen are at my gates.'

The Communion was brief and at its conclusion, any rest Arteche had been considering was forgotten. The college armies were coming. Fast.

Septern allowed himself a smile. Arteche had never to his knowledge been scared by anything. But there was no time to reflect. The victory was insignificant and Septern regretted its necessity. The consequences of the colleges' joint action though were personally enormous.

Switching to the ward grid, Septern let his mind play over the intricate net. As he had been with the chalk map, he was impressed with the level of knowledge the students had developed and the logic they had applied to the maintenance schedule.

Janeth had clearly understood his hints on efficient replenishment and channelling of mana to the static spells. The grid was three quarters fully functional and the balance of the wards was at least operational.

But there were levels and levels of understanding and beneath the grid linkage, where the constructions that triggered the wards to readiness or deployment as others were tripped, lay the real genius. It was something of unique deign and of which Septern was particularly proud. It was not yet perfect – the mana drain in him was still larger than he wanted – but he would get it right. Sometime. He was slightly disappointed that his students had not discovered it but he had to confess that it was well hidden even by his own high standards.

Before Dawnthief it was perhaps his greatest creation yet

one he had not revealed to the mage community at large. There were times when he had wondered why. Now it seemed obvious.

They did not deserve his help.

The mana reservoir was a self-sustaining structure that trapped and fed off what it contained. Focused, uni-directional mana – magical essence ready to fulfil the task of a spell caster without further shaping. It was like a mage carrying an ever brimming barrel of mana on his back. A pity the tap took such an effort to open. His personal stamina would normally be spent in opening the way and replenishing the grid but his students had done greater service than they knew.

The reservoir directed trapped mana in the same way angled mirrors directed light. He had been planning to set up a permanent drain level into the grid to save him from this regular casting but it seemed that opportunity was past.

It was a relatively simple casting to open the tap. The incantation drew life to the feed structures and the delicate hand movements teased open the exact size hole in the reservoir's structure to allow mana to drain at precisely the right rate. Too weak and the process ate up too much stamina, too strong and the wards would be damaged.

Once replenished, Septern activated the border illusions. Should they be breached by any man, horse or dog, every ward in the grid would go live. And from that moment, enough mana power was available to kill tens of thousands. Septern prayed good sense would prevail but knew in his heart that greed and desire would swamp rationality.

He expected blood.

Strange. His belief in the threat of Wesmen and Wytch Lords had led him to lay the grid and make contingency plans for placing any truly powerful spell beyond reach. He had always thought to leave his journals with Dordover so the colleges could trace his genius if he died. Now he knew his enemies were everywhere and there was no one he could trust with his secrets. Not in this dimension.

There was one more task to perform before he could rest. He searched briefly through the mess on his desk, taking a bite of bread and a sip of water in the process, and found a small carved chest two hand-spans long. What it contained was the answer to the question every mage that came after him would ask. It was power absolute in the wrong hands: Septern would make sure it remained in the right ones.

He smiled as he turned the box end over end in his hands. Clumsy carpentry and carving but he had had to try. His enchanting little niece had wanted him to do something 'with no magic' for her seventh birthday. So he had made it for her. Regrettably, plague had claimed her first. At least this way, he would be able to feel he had eventually given her the gift.

He turned, strode to the rip and stepped into its crushing embrace.

)(

Arteche strode past the guards and into the tent of Caltorn, Commander of the Dordovan forces. The General was already irritable due to the abrupt change in his orders and the forced alliance with Xetesk. He was unhappy with supply levels, troop morale, fatigue marching and the increasing number of lame cavalry horses.

Arteche could see his point. This was no way to conduct a war. And they had left the western marches woefully undefended. The cities, though, would have to look after themselves and besides, with reports of Wesmen forces disengaging across the battle front, Arteche had felt confident in the Circle Seven and Dordovan Quorum's decision to head east with everything he could muster. Supplying militia and reserves would have taken weeks. Troops already in the field had been the only option.

Caltorn was instantly awake and reaching for his sword when he saw Arteche and relaxed, a frown stamped across his forehead.

'Gods, man, can't I even rest? What is it now that so urgently demands my attention at whatever ridiculous hour this is?'

'How quickly can we reach the Manse?'

'I accept your apology for waking me,' growled Caltorn.

'How soon?'

'Three days. I have not reassessed the time since we spoke at supper. Now let me sleep.'

'It has to be sooner. Septern will not hold out.' Arteche felt a deep desperation rolling over him as he stared down at the middle-aged general, bald for a decade and never seen to smile.

'Against whom?' The question was spat out but the edge had gone from his hostility.

'The Wesmen hordes will reach the Manse in less than two days. Scouts are already there and Septern's illusions will only hold them until the Wytch Lords divine both them and Septern's signature.'

Caltorn sat up and kneaded at the back of his neck with a muscled hand. 'And the Wytch Lords themselves?'

'In Parve still, so far as our intelligence goes but . . . '

'But it didn't tell you the Wesmen were days ahead of us.' Caltorn nodded.

'Quite,' said Arteche. 'Well?'

'Damn you, Arteche, but this is a disaster waiting to be unleashed.' Caltorn stood and reached for his trousers and shirt. 'I'll do what I can but I will not send exhausted men in to be slaughtered by Wesmen. Make sure your mages are ready to soften them up. I'll take reports from my captains and give you a fresh time. Gods burning but why didn't you hold him at Triverne?'

'I could not act so publicly.'

'And your great spy and assassin network never caught up with him, did it?' Caltorn shook his head. 'You should have left the job to the military.'

Arteche had no answer. Caltorn was right. Had they kept Septern, then the key to Dawnthief would have been in their grasp. Now, the Gods alone knew whose hands it would fall into.

'If we triumph at the Manse, the war will be as good as done,' he said.

'If.' Caltorn held open the flap of his tent and gestured Arteche out. 'Get some sleep, master mage. You and yours are going to need all the stamina you can muster.'

)(

It had been so beautiful. So innocent. And he had led the Kaan straight to it and they, as was the nature of dragons finding a land guarded by a rival brood, had destroyed it.

He remembered the deep blue of the sky above, the lush green of the lands below and the stunning, towering columns that rose thousands of feet to plateaux like the one on which he now stood. There were hundreds of them he had been told, though he could only ever see a handful himself before they were lost in the moist heat haze. He remembered being able to stare down and see clouds below him, and watch the Creaveian at play, flying, tumbling, diving and soaring. Eventually, they had let him join them, his ShadowWings making him one amongst them.

All gone now. All gone because they trusted him and his desire to bring other dimensions to them. What he had brought them, though, was destruction and a long painful slide into death and extinction. And yet still they believed in him and had ever refused to blame him.

The Creaveian. A simple avian race whose language he had learned and with whom he had shared his secrets and his plans. While their existence was the most basic, farming their plateaux and living high on their columns of rock in ovoid dwellings, they understood a good deal about the protection of dimensional space. That was a result of meeting dragons. And when he had discussed with them his closeness to discovering Dawnthief, they had urged him to bring the secret to them, and they had promised to guard it though death take the breath from their bodies and the flesh from their bones. It seemed now they would get their wish. At least the Kaan dragons would make some recompense by guarding the only other key amulet he had made.

He began the walk to the Creaveian village, the rip to his workshop at his back, that to the dragon dimension at the opposite end of the plateau. As always, he skirted the edge of the disc, flirting with the drop. In times gone by, he had gazed down onto the misty green hills and valleys, wondering at the look of predators so effective, they had forced the avians to flee the ground forever. He had also wondered at how long it would be before they developed wings themselves.

But that was an evolution snuffed out. Now all he could see

below him was darkness punctuated by harsh red lightning, while above, impenetrable cloud boiled across the sky on fierce winds. At his level, it was little more than a breeze but the gloom saddened his heart. The Kaan dragons' destruction had blasted dirt high into the atmosphere where it had obscured the sun. They had changed the course of rivers and broken the backs of mountains. And then they had left the remnants of the species that had lived here to die in the perpetual gloom.

Yet the Creaveian had refused his offers of help. He could have taken them back to Balaia, or found a home for them in Beshara, the dragon dimension. But they would not leave, choosing to struggle on in the hope that what the dragons had wrought in their atmosphere and across their lands would subside. There had, of course, never been any hope and Septern felt deep down that many of them knew that and simply accepted the fact that their time had passed.

Approaching the scorched and burned village across the meagre crops that barely survived in this twilight world, Septern could see flutters of movement in some of the dwellings and on the dusty streets between them. There were perhaps seventy Creaveians still alive on this plateau. Maybe others still walked elsewhere but that knowledge was something else denied the survivors. The skies no longer supported their wings and they had forbidden Septern to use magic to bring them information. Their god, they had said, had taken from them the gift of flight and they had to suffer the penance until the gift was returned.

Septern made his way through the village, raising a wave at any he passed. They had little time for talk now, consumed with the desire merely to survive another day. But as he looked on them, he could see death everywhere. Their wings, which had once been glorious rainbows of coloured feathers, were lacklustre and thinning. Their faces, long and oval, bore sunken eyes and drooping mouths; and their limbs were fleshless and weak. Some had even taken to covering themselves against the chill that slowly pervaded the body on these once sun-blessed discs.

Inside a half-fallen dwelling close to the rip to Beshara, a small human child sat quietly, cross legged on the dusty floor. She wore a blue dress with a matching scarf tied around her long blond hair. Her eyes, large and also blue, stared into space, fixing slowly on Septern as he moved towards her to squat on his haunches.

'How's my favourite girl?' he asked softly.

She smiled, her second teeth not all full grown yet and giving her an uneven look. 'I'm all right. It's my birthday soon.'

'I know it is, Lyss. And do you remember what you asked me for?' Septern's voice caught. He knew it wasn't real but tears were gathering behind his eyes.

'Something with no magic,' she said, her cheeks colouring slightly.

'And that's what I've done because you're so special.' He proffered the small chest. 'Look, I made this myself.'

Lyss reached out and took the chest, running her hands over its carvings of leaves and its slightly rough edges.

'Do you like it?' he asked.

Lyss nodded. 'I love it, Uncle Septern. And I love you.'

The tears ran now and he blinked them away, wiping at his cheeks with a hand as well.

'Now, I have something very important to tell you, and you must listen to me. Will you do that?'

Another nod.

'Good girl. I have put something very special in the chest. Something that no one must be allowed to take from you. Only the Kaan may know the secret but even they are not to be fully trusted and that is why you must look after it. Do you understand?'

'Yes. What is it?' Her eyes looked a little frightened now. He stroked one of her arms to comfort her.

'It's a spell I've made up and it can be very dangerous. So no one must cast it.'

'Well why don't you just tear it up?' asked Lyss.

Septern was impressed. It demonstrated acquisitiveness he had not thought possible.

'Because I can't destroy what I have made. I have to leave something behind me for people to remember me by.'

'But they won't know where to look.'

'Ah, but they will look, and that means my name will always be on their lips.'

Septern knew this was beyond the seven year old but it was

not beyond what lay beneath the delicate child's exterior. He stood up and backed away, his dream fulfilled in one small way. The only way open to him.

He gazed down at Lyss, her eyes now locked on the chest again as she studied its lid and fingered the metal clasp. She represented a construct days in preparation. Sentient conjurations were a Xeteskian spell designed to provide a magical guardian that had the wit to report back should it survive whatever task was set for it. The trick was to construct something that would not decay at rest and here, the clearest memory from the casting mage's mind was used. The more complete the memory, the longer lasting the conjuration. And Septern had not forgotten a single detail of Lyss.

She was incongruous with her surroundings he knew, and under the at-rest image was something far darker. That would fulfil the purpose should the need arise.

'Lyss, look at me,' said Septern. 'People are resourceful and one day, some will come. You must not fail. The Creaveians will help you while they can but you must be ready to act on your own. Show me.'

Lyss moved, surging upright. And as she moved, her form changed utterly. Fur burst through skin and fabric, muscles bunched onto arms, hands sprouted long talons. As the dress melted away, a bull chest, thick with coarse hair and with prominent ribs, grew above a packed, hairless stomach. A tail, spiked and leathery, sprouted form the small of her back and her blue eyes shrank to flat black slits, her uneven mouth driving out fangs as it widened. A thin tongue licked out. The beast growled.

'Excellent,' said Septern, noting his nightmare vision was almost exactly as he had envisaged but for the remains of the blond hair which remained high on its head – something else he would have amended if only there had been the more time.

'And should you need to run, where will that be?' he asked.

The creature pointed out of the door and away to the rip towards Beshara.

Septern nodded. 'And whom will you seek?'

'Sha-Kaan,' it said in a voice like falling rocks.

'Your wait may be long. Rest now.'

In moments, Lyss was back, smiling up at him. He leaned in

and kissed her cheek. 'Good bye, Lyss.'

'Good bye, Uncle Septern.'

Swallowing the lump in his throat, he turned and headed back for his workshop and his journal . . . and a few hours of deep, deep sleep.

## Chapter 6

IT WAS LATE afternoon when Septern awoke in his workshop, stretched out on the stone floor, thick blankets below him and a cloak covering him. He could not help but feel a little guilty at his choice of sleeping place. Down in the workshop he was safe from anyone, unlike his students in the rooms above. But when the final analysis came, he had to look after himself until all his work was done. And done it nearly was.

He gave a long stretch and rolled his shoulders as he got to his feet, feeling stiff but refreshed, a spell having kept him asleep in his rather uncomfortable surroundings. He cast a weak LightGlobe to illuminate the dark of the workshop, with only the rip casting any luminescence at all, and even that feeble and shifting.

Walking over to his desk, he looked down at the entry he had written in a sudden swathe of despair and managed a weak smile. The concluding paragraph was desperate and, after his hours of rest, he felt considerably brighter.

*'For myself, having hidden what had to be hidden, I must destroy the rip, closing the door forever. To do so, I must remain on this side and will take my own life. No one must find Dawnthief. No one.'*

Strong words although, while he agreed with their sentiment, the refreshing sleep and his consequent better humour made him feel that perhaps there was a less drastic solution. There had to be a way to dismantle the rip from the plateau. All it would require was a little thought and some time. And surely, hidden in his workshop, he would have that. The Wytch Lords would divine him eventually but, while he would always retain the option of suicide, he was confident that he could escape.

Now, though, he had to return to the reality that was the Manse. Clutching the amulet, he uttered the short incantation and the door opened to the drawing room. Relief at the quiet he heard cascaded through him. Indeed in addition to the fact that there were no sounds of battle, it was possible his students were still asleep. But when he clambered up the ladder, they were waiting for him.

Septern closed the workshop quickly and faced the quartet of angry faces.

'You had no right,' said Janeth. 'You left us helpless. We could all have been murdered in our beds while you hid in safety.'

'But you are not dead. You are all very much alive and very much refreshed.'

'You played with our lives, Master Septern,' said Sandor.

Septern bit back his first reply, nodding instead and holding his hands up in apology.

'I understand your anger. But don't judge me without all of the facts. Please, follow me outside.' They looked back blankly. 'Please.'

Eventually, Janeth shrugged and gestured Septern to lead them into the grounds.

He said nothing as he walked out of the front door, drank in the warmth of the late afternoon sun and headed for the northern edge of the grounds. They passed lawns and an ornamental pond that gave way to a kitchen garden and then fallow fields. Fences marked areas for grass and crops and beyond that, the land was left wild for the sheep Septern had been planning to buy as he moved towards self-sufficiency.

Beyond his grounds, the land was less fertile as it tracked north to thinner soils, tough shrub, woodland and stark, barren hills. He could see the movement well before they reached the illusion's edge and heard Sandor mutter something behind him. About twenty yards from the boundary, he stopped and let them take in what they saw.

Tents had been erected, fires burned and voices travelled the space. The Wesmen were massing. Where he had seen the trio of scouts, there were now perhaps two thousand of the Wesman vanguard, creating the camp from which they would launch their attack. The invaders knew they were close but would also know that magic kept them from seeing their prize; and Wesmen were fearful enough of magic to wait for direction.

'They're *here*,' said Dirrion.

Septern turned. 'Yes. Our time is very short. Their numbers will grow in the next few hours and then all they are awaiting are orders from the Wytch Lords. The illusions will be breached moments later and our jobs will begin in earnest. Arteche is another day away at least and we have to hold out until the armies collide.'

It was an unworldly experience. For all their knowledge of spells and the power of magic, all five of them felt the same. They looked at the Wesmen as if through a one way glass of some kind. The nearest tent was less than a hundred yards away and Septern had no doubt the scouts knew there were illusions around them. He had equal confidence that the Wesmen's fear was such that they would move no further without a horde behind them.

He turned and saw a look pass between Janeth and Sandor that he did not understand.

'Is something wrong?' he asked.

Janeth shook his head. 'No.' His face cleared and he smiled.

'Don't you see? You were exhausted. You would not have been capable of helping me in the fight against them unless you had rested. And your minds were in such a turmoil that real rest was the last thing you would seek. I know your strengths and that you would have resisted me however unconsciously. I had no choice.'

There was a brief silence.

'What I was going to say,' said Janeth. 'Was that we owe you an apology. We should have trusted your judgement.'

Now it was Septern's turn to smile. 'In this matter, perhaps. But my judgement has been shown to be lacking elsewhere.' He indicated the gathering Wesmen.

'We shall prevail,' said Sandor.

'Excellent,' said Septern. 'Now, we need to organise

ourselves to eat and then, if I may, I would like to instruct you on how we can best handle what is about to engulf us.'

He ushered his students back to the Manse.

♓

'What will you do, Master Septern?' asked Thuneron the next morning at breakfast.

An eerie calm had settled on the Manse. A dawn walk had revealed the Wesmen numbers swelled on the north side to somewhere in the region of ten thousand with a similar force gathered to the south west. They were readying for battle, that much was clear but were looking outward as well as inward. They knew the colleges were coming.

It had been almost possible to forget what might happen at any moment. Sandor had busied himself in the kitchen while his fellows laid the table and the chink of china and cutlery gave the situation a surreal quality.

'There's a good deal of work to be done before any decision can be made. Dawnthief is hidden and perhaps the colleges will see their action will gain nothing. In any event, you will be safe returned to the bosom of our mage masters.' Septern mentally crossed his fingers that that would indeed be the case. 'But, if the Wesmen should be pounding on the doors, escape will be the only option. For all of us.'

'You would take us with you through the rip?' Dirrion gaped.

'I came back here to see you live. I could hardly leave and let you die. But let us hope it doesn't come to that.'

'I'm sure it won't,' said Janeth.

Septern raised his eyebrows, his confidence of the previous evening now eroded by the sheer numbers gathering at his borders. 'Belief like yours, all of you, shames me.'

He stared around the table and saw such a conflict of emotions. Dirrion and Thuneron both were fearful yet too proud to let that fear gain hold. No doubt they took strength from Janeth and Sandor, both of whom looked as if they were about to indulge in a bit of simple research rather than in all probability fight for their

65

lives. He found their confidence a little unnerving if he were honest. It was a trait he had readily recognised within himself at other times. Perhaps he had taught them too well.

'The wonders we would see,' said Dirrion, mind still lost in another dimension.

'Yes,' agreed Septern. 'But bear in mind you would not be able to return unless you were able to master dimensional magics yourself. I will not build a rip back to Balaia. We would be five alone in alien lands. Dangerous lands.'

'An adventure worth the sacrifice,' said Dirrion.

Septern nodded. He knew he had been right to choose this quartet. Perhaps they were not geniuses in his own mould but they had that driving sense to explore and learn that had led him to push out from his own dimension.

'Perhaps we should all travel with you anyway,' said Thuneron.

'Perhaps you won't be given the opportunity,' replied Septern. 'You still have a great deal to learn and here is the best place.'

'Without you?'

Septern shrugged. 'Anyone can teach you the basics you still lack. But let's not dwell on what might happen. Are you all comfortable with what I have asked you to do?'

They all indicated they were.

'Then you, Dirrion, why are you not tuned in to the illusion structures? I don't want to know there has been a breach when the first ward explodes. And you, Janeth, your skills at eating boiled eggs are complete. Perhaps you should ready yourself to channel mana to parts of the grid that come under the most stress.' He swept them with his gaze again. 'Do I have to say more?'

Chairs scraped on the floor, a flurry of limbs, knives dropped to plates, last gulps taken from coffee cups. Septern leaned back in his chair and chuckled . . . instantly in charge again But though he was still respected for his every word and deed, he had better enjoy it while he could.

'Remember!' he called after them. 'I will centre the effort and signal you through a split Communion. Pass messages through me, I shall be open to you all.'

This was not a battle that would be fought in the field, sword in hand. It would be fought prone, each student lying relaxed on his bed while Septern sat in his favourite leather armchair in front of the great bay windows in the drawing room that faced south and caught the sun all day long.

He walked quickly to his position, settling himself to look out over a rolling shrub-edged lawn that led to the stream that bordered his gardens. It was beautiful. A shame the waters would soon be running with blood.

He closed his eyes and tapped into the mana spectrum, focusing on the trails of the ward grid, pulsing strong and sure. Around them, the spikes of his students circled, confident and clear, their minds watching and waiting. He had trained them well.

Opening his mind completely, Septern shaped a Communion. It was a risk. He had let his own mind shield lapse. It was the only way to allow his students to speak with him without losing their own concentration. Should an enemy realise his vulnerability, he could be killed in an instant.

'Janeth, can you hear me?'

'Yes Master Septern.'

'Do not be distracted. I shall guide you. Remember what I have promised to you.'

'Yes.'

'Sandor, is your mind calm?'

'It is, Master Septern.'

'Good. Beware stamina drain. Coax the power, do not drive it.'

'I will Master, thank you.'

'Dirrion, is the illusion border secure?'

'Yes, Master Septern. There is no breach.'

'As soon as a body touches it, you will know. Pass the grid reference through me. Do not hesitate. You can then take up your secondary task.'

'I understand.'

'Thuneron. Do you have the repeaters in your sight?'

'All of them, Master Septern.'

'Excellent. Remember, if any structures should falter, close them down. There is a backfire risk to your mind. Maintain what you can. They are the bedrock of our defence.'

'I won't let you down.'

'I know.'

Septern was satisfied. At the centre of the operation, he could talk to one in turn or all at once. It would be a fascinating experiment if nothing else. In his plans, he had always been alone when the ward grid was breached and the sheer weight of numbers were to give him the time to escape with what he needed from the house. Now though, there was a chance significant parts of the grid would remain active through wards being protected and reset after initial triggering.

That would give the Wesmen pause for thought. Or he hoped it would. He breathed deep, scanned the grid another time and relaxed into the wait.

$$)($$

Arteche flew high over the Wesmen armies, flitting in and out of the thin cloud layer. He knew they would see him and hate him but he was safe. Around him, three dozen mages trailed the skies to the north of the Manse, logging everything they saw to take back to Caltorn and the swiftly approaching Dordovan and Xeteskian forces.

What he could see worried him deeply. The Wesmen were building and waiting. He could see an attack was imminent and his ground troops were still a day away. To the south, the situation was just as grave but for different reasons. The Wesmen did not seem quite as organised and, potentially worse, the Julatsans were fast approaching. Lystern was trailing in their wake and would provide no serious threat. But should the Julatsans break the Wesmen line, they could reach the Manse before him, assuming their divination of Septern's ward grid was up to it – and he had no reason to believe it wasn't.

That was a situation that would have to be monitored and like it or not, Caltorn would have to be prepared to split his forces and take on the other college if the time came. Unpalatable when they were facing a common enemy but Balaian dominion was at stake.

He circled the extremes of Septern's grounds, marvelling at the skill the rogue mage displayed in everything he did. The knitting of the multiple illusions was perfect and he found himself believing in them despite his absolute knowledge of what he was seeing. That was the measure of the man's ability and for the first time, Arteche was afforded an inkling of the feelings of the average Wesman.

They would be aware of what faced them – that they could not necessarily trust their own eyes and that beyond what they suspected might be illusion but were too fearful to touch, was more and more magic against which they had no defence. Hardly surprising therefore, that the tribes from the west of the Blackthorne Mountains were at best wary of magic and at worst running scared. Small wonder they waited for Wytch Lord orders and drive before moving again. The Wesmen were masters at fighting what they could see and understand, and hopeless when faced with enemies unseen.

It was fortunate, then, that Dordover and Xetesk were not.

Arteche swept back over the northern approaches, noting more activity below. He swept lower, breath catching in his throat. Around the edges of the growing encampment, Wesmen horse lords galloped, their banner men behind them, pennants splashes of colour against the greens and browns. And everywhere they galloped, Wesmen tribesmen surged to their feet, their cries and songs reverberating across the space, the roar reaching up to and beyond the flying mage. So quickly, they banded and formed up by tribe and just as quickly, with an echo of orders, they ran full tilt at the dense forest ahead, beyond which, they would see Septern's Manse.

Arteche raced around, dropped lower still and tracked in a hundred feet over the heads of the Wesmen, bracing himself for what he was about to witness and feeling, despite himself, a small pang of sorrow for the tribesmen running headlong to certain death.

He held his breath as he chased through the illusion, ever that mote of doubt that he was wrong and would impale himself on a pine branch but then he was through and in a brief instant of peace, the immediate battleground was laid out before him. A battleground in which he would only ever see one side.

The Manse was half a mile distant over a peaceful range of fields, lawns, a pond and decorative gardens. Inside it, somewhere, were Septern and his unfortunate students. A strange quartet, that lot – ignoring attempts at Communion from Dordover . . . undoubtedly as a result of some distorted sense of loyalty. Septern's students often displayed that and, grateful though Dordover was that he taught them so supremely well, the Quorum could ever do without the attitude that came with it.

Arteche accelerated well ahead of the Wesmen and turned to watch them pour over the lip of the illusion. In an instant, the world was turned to fire.

Scant feet inside the grounds, a wall of fire four hundred yards wide and fifty feet high gorged from the earth, its flames tinted with Dordovan deep blue. It engulfed the first lines of Wesmen as they ran, the magical flames eating cloth and flesh, Arteche feeling the sudden surge in heat from where he hovered in relative safety. Their momentum carrying them on, burning warriors ploughed ahead, tripping ward after ward as they came. A series of explosions ripped across the line, sending up great clumps of mud and rock, the flash of the detonations momentarily blinding, the screams of the Wesmen cut off as hundreds were blown apart, gore scattering over the fields, fence posts shattering.

Still they came on but the charge was already faltering. The wall of fire had died from its power peak but still it savaged those it touched and Arteche could see burning Wesmen rolling in the dirt or running back into their kin as panic took hold. A second series of explosions shattered the late morning air, wind whipped across the Wesmen lines. The managust picked men from their feet and flung them back high over the heads of those following, chased by yet more blue-tinged fire that had the sharper in the charge diving and rolling as it scorched over their heads to thunder into those not so quick.

Disorder rippled through the advancing Wesmen and in their thousands, they pulled up and stopped, ignoring the exhortations of their lords sitting safe on horseback behind them. Across the line, Wesmen turned to run back and the momentum was lost. Almost immediately, the fire wall died to nothing, peace reined again and Arteche nodded his approval. He rose high, span through the upper illusion layer and sped back towards Caltorn, able to report at least a modicum of good news.

## Chapter 7

DIRRION FELT A tremor through the mana spectrum centred on the illusion structures. His eyes sought and found agitation in the constructs marking the northern borders and his sense told him a significant attack had begun.

'Driving in north to south. Two hundred wide,' he said, feeling his heart start to hammer. He fought the sudden urge to run to the window and watch the attempted invasion but swallowed it back, Septern's words calming him further.

'Thank you, Dirrion. Beware of backwash in the illusion constructs from tripped wards.'

Septern had felt the imminent attack and had traced the likely path already. If ever the Wesmen decided on subtlety, they might be dangerous. Every ward was live but not every direction was perfect.

'Sandor, trim the FireCliff. Angle a few degrees west.'

'I understand.'

'Janeth, prepare. Let the traps trigger as normal but wrap around to maintain the structures. Keep them together.'

'Understood.'

'Thuneron, direct flow from sector east one. Keep those traps running with minimal inflow until I say otherwise.'

'I'll try.'

'Do better than that,' snapped Septern.

He was glad he did not have to see it. He monitored the triggering of the FireCliff and felt the reverberations as the first traps detonated. Moments later, the sound wave rattled the windows and shook dust from high shelves.

The trap structures – which normally shredded as the ward was tripped – held firm, coaxed by Janeth's skilful, focused ministrations.

'Increase the flow, Thuneron. Let's have them again.'

'Yes, Master.'

In came the mana, charging the traps that dealt out instant explosive carnage.

'Janeth, on my word,' said Septern.

'As ever,' drawled Janeth, voice a little strained with concentration.

It was perfect. The charge streaming in, the structure solid and held off-line by his star student. Then, an idea.

'Let's adjust the detail,' said Septern. 'Janeth, turn the structure's upper helix to a flat cone throughout. Don't disrupt any other part. That would be bad.'

'I - '

'There's never a wrong time to learn. Trust me. Just concentrate. You can do it. On one first, then replicate. Section your mind.'

Septern let his mind flow over the trap ward shapes as they adjusted. Not a fleck of mana was wasted in the process.

'Excellent. Release.'

Janeth did, and this time the wind would slap by the advancing Wesmen, followed by a gout of flame hotter than a dragon's breath. It would melt bone.

'Agitation reversing in signature,' said Dirrion. 'They're turning back.'

'Excellent, gentlemen. Tune out the FireCliff, Sandor. Let's maintain, check and balance. Remember the simple things. Leave the grid active then relax. Well done, everyone.'

Impressive. Septern had to admit it was very, very impressive. And so simple. Merely a monitoring and redirection of mana. But to do the simple, you had to see the possibility first. He hoped his students would learn something from this.

Confident the short barrage would stop the Wesmen for a while at least, Septern dismissed the open Communion, tuned his eyes and mind out of the mana spectrum and took in the beauty of the day.

Behind him, to the north of the Manse, the destruction would be awful, blood running into the earth and charred bodies lying as grotesque markers to the power of magic over man. But here, the serenity was unbroken despite the knowledge of another force not a mile away.

Of course, what they had done was not strictly necessary. Leaving the wards to do their work would have brought the same result. But it proved to Septern what he had expected all along: that structures could be protected within an explosive environment – given a mage of suitable ability – and that genuine co-operation in an open mind situation could achieve pretty much anything.

It was something worth noting for the colleges, though he wondered why he felt the need to give them anything. Force of habit, he supposed; and the belief that not every mage would support their college's action.

Deciding he probably had time to scribble a few notes in the main workshop, he pushed himself to his feet and turned to find Janeth and Sandor watching him from just inside the door. Despite himself, he started.

'I didn't hear you come in.'

'No,' said Janeth. 'That was the idea.'

'I appreciate your concern but I wasn't casting.'

'It wouldn't have mattered either way,' said Sandor.

'Oh, I see,' said Septern, though he did not. Thinking he woud talk to them about it later, he switched subjects to keep himself focused. 'Tell me, Sandor, what you thought of our work just now?'

Sandor raised his eyebrows. 'Interesting. It demonstrated a feature we had not previously considered.'

'And that's why you're here. To learn to consider that which others would not.' Septern smiled. 'I had thought to make a few notes to crystallise our understanding. After all, we have no guarantee of such success another time. I would welcome your input.'

Sandor turned to Janeth. 'Is there time?'

'For that? Yes, I should think so,' he replied.

'Oh, I don't think the Wesmen will regroup in too much of a hurry after that bloody nose,' said Septern.

74

'No,' said Janeth. 'But let's write in here. Sandor will fetch parchment for you.'

'A pleasure.' The farmer's son hurried out of the drawing room.

Septern watched him go. 'Thank you. Would you call the others?'

'That isn't necessary. Dirrion wanted to watch the boundaries and Thuneron is resting. Let's leave them be.'

Septern nodded. He knew them well enough already to see the hierarchy amongst them. And this wasn't the time to challenge it.

'Excellent. Let's sit then and be comfortable.'

He gestured to the desk, with its single, leather upholstered and high-backed chair behind and two plain stools in front. 'We can't be too long over this. The Wesmen will not wait forever.'

'Absolutely,' said Janeth. 'And we must be ready.'

'Yes.' Septern half paused as he moved. There was something . . . He shook his head. It was probably nothing.

He settled himself into his chair, inked a quill and scribbled on a blotter to check its edge. Sandor trotted back in with a sheaf of flat parchment and placed it on the desk.

'Excellent. First I will write my thoughts. If you have anything to add at anytime, do so. If not, once I am finished I will ask for your individual perspectives. Let's begin.'

Septern bent his head and began to write, speaking aloud each word as the quill scratched its mark. He wrote quickly, aware that time was short but comfortable in the knowledge that Dirrion would give them at least some early warning of another incursion before the wards began to trip anew.

For whatever reason, he found concentration a little difficult. He was accurate enough in his work but it seemed hard to find exactly the right words and, all too often, he scored out a phrase and rewrote. He would have to copy it up again, assuming he had time.

Sandor and Janeth said nothing the whole time. Indeed, he hardly heard them draw breath. He was used to being watched with something akin to awe but these two really should know better by now. Yet their eyes never left him, he could feel them boring into the top of his skull and he had to deny the urge to scratch his head.

Strange, but perhaps they were suffering a reaction to what they had done. None of them had killed men before and despite not having to face their victims, the knowledge was there nonetheless. Septern would admit to a sour taste in his mouth and a sense of unease despite this not having been his first kill, and of course his students were but inexperienced youths. He trusted they would be rational enough to accept the need while not necessarily enjoying the actions themselves.

Septern finished his outline and detail, marked the parchment with his signature and laid the quill on the blotter, reading over the last couple of paragraphs. Satisfied, he looked up and there they were, watching him with a kind of detached half-interest as if they were both consumed with something else. Quite possibly they were scared of what was beyond the edges of the ward grid and of what they had wrought so casually. It would be quite understandable.

'Don't worry,' he said. 'We'll be gone from here long before any Wesmen can truly threaten us.'

Janeth blinked. 'Pardon? Oh, yes. Absolutely. I know.'

'Concentration, Janeth. It will ever be your curse unless you tame it and practise it.' Septern shook his head. 'Now. Assuming you've been listening at least, what do you think of my assessment?'

'Excellent,' said Sandor in a passable impersonation of Septern, who smiled.

'Very, very useful,' said Janeth.

'I hope so,' replied Septern. 'For it not to be would be an affront to magic and a monumental waste of time. And do you have anything to add before I ask you some questions?'

'Yes,' said Janeth.

And Sandor rose, reached across the table and grabbed Septern's robes at the neck.

'This is all very well. But we want Dawnthief. Now.'

Sandor's first punch had Septern's head spinning.

)(

Dirrion lay relaxed as Septern had always demanded, his mind open to the nuances of the mana flow, his consciousness able to pluck the vital information from the mass.

The illusion boundaries were quiet and unruffled, the Wesmen stung badly and no doubt assessing their next action. Further, much further, he could sense the frenetic activity of hundreds of magical minds as the combined Dordovan and Xeteskian armies approached. Dirrion was badly scared. He felt such a weight of responsibility on his shoulders. There was no one else monitoring the borders or the grid. The Wesmen could come across at any moment and Janeth had minded him to be sure his concentration didn't slip.

Despite the brief euphoria of the early victory, Dirrion could not lift the gloom from his mind. They should have run while they had the chance. And now the Wesmen were practically battering on his bedroom door and the college armies were still so far away.

He didn't want to spend his life living in another dimension. He loved Balaia. Why had he listened to Sandor and Janeth? No courage. No real belief. Not like them. If he *had* he been, he would have left, knowing it was right. But he was weak in all but pure magic.

At least he could gain succour there. None of them could match his speed of learning and acquisition of lore. They were all slow – even Septern said so. But then again, so what if he had to spend his life in an alien land? It was better than being slaughtered as he lay on his bed.

A movement in the mana trails brought him back to himself in an instant. There it was again, a pushing at the edges of the illusions, as if a hand were pressing on the constructs. He could imagine it only too clearly. Wesman fingers inching through, praying that no explosion followed.

They were coming back. Slowly, but they *were* coming.

'Thuneron, call them back,' he said, his voice loud enough to carry through the open door to the next room. 'I have to keep watch. Call the others to cast, the Wesmen are coming.'

No reply. His concentration slipped and he almost lost the ManaMeld that kept him hovering above the grid.

'Thuneron!' he called. 'Answer me! Please.'

Nothing. And now his heart beat too fast, his breath

dragged sharply into his lungs and he was wrenched from the mana spectrum. The real world swam into view with a sickening whirl. He could hear nothing around him. No action, no urgency. No one had heard him.

'Gods, Thuneron, what the hell are you playing at?'

He lurched to his feet, blood rushing, threatening to steal him to a faint. He steadied himself briefly, panic pounding through him.

'The Wesmen!' he shouted to anyone that would hear as he ran to the door to Thuneron's room. 'The Wes - '

It took him a moment to take in what he saw. And in the same instant that he realised it was blood that covered the sheets on which Thuneron lay with his neck slashed apart, the advancing Wesmen tripped the first wards once again. But this time, no one was there to protect and recharge them.

Not sure if it was the sight or the thought that scared him more, Thuneron ran screaming for the only man who could save him.

Septern.

)(

He knew what they were doing. Draining his stamina. Causing him pain that would damage his concentration. Sap his strength and stop him from casting. It was the classic way to subdue a mage. What they couldn't afford to do was kill him, or let him kill himself, before they had Dawnthief.

For a confused moment, reeling under Sandor's heavy punches, he had assumed they wanted the spell for themselves. But it wasn't that. And he had cursed himself for not seeing the blindingly obvious before he even arrived back at the Manse.

He dragged himself back to his feet and wiped a hand across his mouth, fighting back a sweep of nausea from the latest blow. Sandor's punches and kicks had fallen like rain into his midriff and lower back. His gut and kidneys ached and throbbed, and his head swam with the pain. They almost had him where they wanted him. *Almost.*

Sandor stood over him, the jovial expression replaced by

one of determined contempt. It saddened Septern to see the change in him but it was like a knife in the heart to see Janeth's expression. That was hatred.

Septern waited for the next blow but it never came. Sandor stepped back at a word from Janeth, the two standing shoulder to shoulder, close enough to react if he began to cast.

'I'm disappointed they got to you so easily,' said Septern. 'I thought better of you.'

Janeth raised his eyebrows. '"Got to us?" I don't follow.' There was the ghost of a smile on his face.

Septern shuddered, clutching at his stomach as he fought to stand straight and unsupported, his back to the bay windows, the sunlight glorious.

'The Dordovans, Arteche. When did they pierce the shield here? Three days ago? Four? The day I left?' He spat those last words, furious at the betrayal, at the waste of his teaching, his spirit and, more than all of those, his time. They were not worthy of him.

'We've had no contact with Dordover since we left to come here,' said Janeth. 'Strange, isn't it? You're so clever in the ways of magic. So valuable to us. And yet so blind. Now, open the workshop door and bring us Dawnthief.'

Septern's confusion deepened again. Either they were lying or they were working for another college. The only thing certain was that they were in a hurry to get the spell because the Wesmen wanted it for the Wytch Lords. The balance tipped just a little.

Septern pulled the amulet from inside his shirt and began to walk towards the centre of the drawing room, the two students moving aside to let him pass, their eyes shining with victory. Premature. Septern turned to face them, swinging the amulet gently on its chain.

'Haven't studied here long enough have you?' He enjoyed watching doubt's shadow cross their faces. 'I would have taught you the basics of four college lore to be able to read this amulet and then you wouldn't have needed me would you? But now you can't get the spell without me because you can't understand how to get into the workshop. Poor boys.'

Janeth's face clouded and he advanced until he stood so close their noses almost touched.

'And we would have waited and we would have learned. Just as we waited and learned your ward grid. But you had to go and announce Dawnthief, didn't you? And then the time was gone and now the colleges are almost at the gates.'

Septern took a pace back so he could see Janeth clearly. 'The colleges? I would worry more about the Wesmen if I were you.'

Janeth laughed. 'So blind, clever Septern. The Wesmen are no threat. To you maybe . . . but never to us.'

The strength left Septern then and he staggered, almost falling but never taking his eyes from those who faced him. These two fresh faced youths. Eager and intelligent. And agents of the Wytch Lords.

Outside a flash brighter than the sun was followed by an explosion that rattled the windows. Upstairs, a man screamed. The Wesmen were attacking and everything changed.

.

# Chapter 8

FOOTSTEPS RATTLED ON the stairs in the hall beyond the drawing room door. Sandor paced quickly across.

'I'll deal with him,' he said.

'Your friends are coming again,' said Septern, ignoring him and turning to Janeth, sensing a slight chance now the two were split. 'The same ones you killed so easily a short time ago. And you can't save these ones. I will not disable the grid.'

Janeth shrugged. 'They are many and expendable. And what we learned from you was more valuable than a few primitive lives.'

A series of detonations shook the foundations. Alarms shrieked across the grounds, flame lashed at the air and beyond it, Septern felt he could hear the Wesmen's cries.

'Worried they'll get here or worried they won't?' said Septern. 'Your Masters sent them here to bring you and the spell back, did they not? Looks to me as though you are running out of time. And the colleges are so very close.'

Janeth backhanded Septern across the face. 'The workshop, Septern. *Now.*'

Septern shook his head. 'Kill me and fail. You haven't the wit to succeed, boy.'

The drawing room door slapped open and Dirrion charged in, his face pale beneath his freckles, his eyes wide and terrified.

'Master Septern, Thuneron's been - '

Sandor caught the smaller youth easily around the chest, swept him in to a crushing embrace and snapped his neck with a sharp twist of his other arm.

' – murdered,' said the farmer's son as he dropped the corpse to the ground. 'And the Wesmen are coming.'

He turned to Septern and smiled.

Septern said nothing but inside he snapped. Swinging round, he landed a punch clear on Janeth's face that cracked his nose and sent him sprawling away, crashing into the chairs that sat around the desk.

Sandor reacted quickly, moving fast from the doorway. Septern's chosen spell was quick but it was a gamble. He held it in, the shape strong, its flared conical structure spinning and turning in his mind. As the younger man closed to bring him down, Septern reached out his right hand, palm flat to push against Sandor's face.

He took the impact, clinging to his concentration with every fibre of his being and as the two of them flew to the ground, his hand found its target, the FlamePalm firing out of its centre, the super-heated mana essence slapping into Sandor's face, burning away his lips, gouting up his nose and driving into his eyes.

Sandor screamed, his grip slackened and he rolled away, clutching at his ruined face, the flame still clawing its way in. It would expend itself soon; FlamePalm was not a powerful range spell and designed for nothing more than fire-lighting but Sandor would be dead before it did.

Septern turned away from the blackening mess, the smell of seared flesh in his nostrils and stood up, trying to ignore the wails of agony that even now were lessening as Sandor slipped towards unconsciousness. He faced Janeth, hearing as if in the distance more wards tripping and triggering. More death outside. And he had brought it all on. The Wesmen wouldn't reach them yet. Maybe not ever. Whatever, it would be too late for the Wytch Lords.

'Just you and me now,' said Septern, trying to ignore the pain in his hand from the backwash of the FlamePalm but knowing it would seriously hamper him in casting another quick spell. Janeth's face was covered in blood and he was unsteady on his feet but he advanced nonetheless.

'That was a very bad mistake, Septern. The Masters had great plans for Sandor.'

'And now they will have to make new plans without either of you and without Dawnthief. Where are they now, eh, Janeth?

Something this important and they send boys and defenceless tribesmen after Balaia's best mage? I wonder if they really ever expected you to succeed.'

Janeth moved forward still, one hand wiping blood from his mouth as it poured out of his smashed nose. Outside, the wards were quiet, the Wesmen beaten back again. Clouds of smoke carried on the breeze past the window, momentarily dimming the bright sunlight.

'We have had students with you for a decade and more, Septern. All of us just waiting for you to unlock the secret you have always craved. I was merely the fortunate one. It is my road to power in Balaia far greater than you could possibly conceive.'

Septern's heart missed a beat at that though he realised immediately he shouldn't have been surprised. He wondered briefly who among his earlier students had been a spy for the Wytch Lords. Perhaps one day he would take the time to figure it out. First, though, he had to survive.

'It didn't have to come to this, Janeth. I had such hopes for you. But rather than develop as the man to take on my work long after I have gone, you are now going to be just another life wasted by the Wytch Lords.'

Janeth managed a smile. 'A broken nose is not a fatal injury, Septern. And the Wesmen will not harm me. Neither will the colleges. After all, am I not just an innocent caught up in your arrogant folly? I'll be safe enough here. It is you who will die and I who will take the amulet to my Masters. Its language will be simple for them, I'm sure.'

'Poor Janeth,' said Septern. 'You really think you can beat me? We are both hampered by injury but you are just a puppy. I am the true master and I always will be.'

But Janeth only laughed, drew a dagger from within his robes and plunged it into Septern's chest. Septern gasped and fell back a pace, the blade wrenching clear, a dull ache spreading across his body, white hot pain at the wound point.

'I have no intention of taking you on in a spell dual, Septern. Idiot. There may be honour in it but there's certainly no gain.'

He came on again, the dagger raised. Septern saw it all with uncommon clarity, the dagger glinting in the light, his blood slick on its surface, held high as Janeth came at him. He did the only thing open to him, he kicked out straight and hard, Janeth seeing the blow coming, his blade arm arrowing downwards but missing.

Septern's foot slapped clean into Janeth's groin and the youth collapsed, wind gone, dagger dropped from nerveless hands that clutched between his legs as he retched violently. Septern stepped in and lashed a foot into Janeth's face again and again, his head rapping on the ground, his eyes glazing but his mind clinging on to consciousness. Dark blood ran from his cracked skull in a torrent.

The Balaian master mage knelt down by the crumpled form and cupped his chin in one hand, the other pressed into his own chest over the wound that had surely punctured a lung.

'And now you will learn another lesson. One that I could have taught you in less chastened circumstances had you kept faith with me rather than the bastard sons of Balaia.' Janeth struggled feebly, one hand clutching at Septern's arm but it was easily thrown off. His eyes, though dimmer, still held their hate. 'There are two hundred wards anchored to the wood and stone of this house as I think you are aware. And all face out to keep those within safe. Unfortunately for you, I no longer have the strength to hold off the Wesmen by charging the outer grid so I will have to leave the dimension now. But I can't leave any clues, can I?

'Here's the lesson. In integral part of a successful ward is a small construct that determines direction. It is a segmented circle at the base of each one. One great advantage of having an integral linkage in the structure of the house wards is that with one small casting, the direction of them all can be very easily changed. I will demonstrate. Inwards might be good.' He pushed Janeth's head back and sneered down at him. 'Fascinating magic, don't you agree?'

Septern had little time. Rising to his feet he coughed a spray of blood and felt a shooting agony through his chest. He paced backwards, his free hand grabbing for the amulet, his mind already trying to form the shape to open the workshop trapdoor. It wasn't a solid form, his head was swimming with the pain in his gut, kidneys and now chest threatening suddenly to overwhelm him.

'Calm,' he whispered to himself. 'Calm.'

The construct steadied a little, perhaps enough. He mouthed the command word and heard the slight thud as the dimension door opened behind him.

Janeth was moving again, dragging himself to his haunches, his face covered in blood, his head weaving as he sought to focus, one hand still clamped over his groin. Septern's heart beat faster and his vision dimmed momentarily, slick red pulsing between his fingers.

He turned and headed for the opening and the ladder, his whole body shaking now with the effort, his breath shortening. He had to rest but not yet. Not yet. Not daring to descend forwards, he knelt and searched with a foot for the first rung, his eyes fixed on Janeth who moved in a terrible slow half crawl towards him, every movement a life-threatening effort, his shoulders red, his skin paling almost visibly. But on he came. Inexorable, driven by the desire to live and to win, driven by dreams of glory and power. Septern could understand that all right.

Descending as fast as he could, Septern slumped at the bottom of the ladder and tried to tune into the mana spectrum and the house ward grid, unable to shut the trapdoor before he did so. The workshop was in inter-dimensional space; he needed the link to the Balaian dimension for just a few moments more.

Above him, he could hear Janeth dragging his body over the stone flags. His head span as he tried to adjust his mind to the mana. It wouldn't come. For a dozen agonising heartbeats it wouldn't come; and all the time his ears picked up the rasp of Janeth's breath and the drag of his feet.

At last, another moment of pure clarity and the grid was laid out before him, its lines pulsing, its ward structures active, coiling, spinning or glowing with suppressed, trapped power. With a deft move of his hand, he altered the pitch of one, small segmented circle. Deep blue mana flared briefly along the grid lines. Above him, Janeth moved again.

And tripped a ward.

A low alarm wail echoed out in the drawing room above him. Septern snapped out of the mana spectrum and dismissed the shape holding the trap door open. As it snapped back into place, plunging him into total darkness and silence, he thought he heard Janeth scream . . . perhaps for mercy.

)(

He almost got there. His fingers were that close to the edge of the hole in the floor. He knew he was dying but he only had to grab the amulet and he would have won. He dragged himself on another foot, whimpering as the movement sent extraordinary pain down every nerve from his shattered skull.

An alarm ward was triggered. For a heartbeat, he thought it was outside but, dragging his head around to look through the window, he knew it was too loud and too close. The chain reaction had begun. All he could do was watch as the glass thundered inwards and the flame rolled across the drawing room. Its heat blistered his skin and cindered his clothes. The glass slivered the flesh from his face and tore out his eyes.

But at the very end, the pain disappeared and he was at peace.

)(

Arteche alone had followed the second Wesmen attack as it came in, watched them advance double the distance before turning back again, leaving their dead and injured littering the ground. This time, the wards had not repeated and he knew the Wesmen sensed it too. Something was wrong.

The defenceless tribesmen had suffered enormously in their first attack, triggering wards which then, contrary to all known magic, triggered again. You had to hand it to Septern, there really was nothing he could not do.

Yet the Wesmen had regrouped and come again, driven by their lust for victory, their terror of the Wytch Lords, and their fear of failure in battle. And now they had made ground.

Arteche decided to circle the Manse. He wasn't sure he would see anything but any clue, no matter how small, might help his mages when they came to tackle Septern once the Wesmen armies were pushed back. Flying just under the illusory canopy, Arteche arrowed in, passing across a low barn and other outbuildings, a stable block and yard.

No more than a hundred yards from the north facing wall, he felt a great surge in the mana around him, as if it were being sucked into a vortex emanating from within the Manse itself. Clinging desperately to the shape of his ShadowWings as the pull threatened to steal his concentration and send him plunging to the earth, he wheeled away and up fast, hearing the unmistakable wail of an alarm ward below him.

He banked round, came to a hover and searched the grounds for the incursion but no Wesman was within the borders that he could see. The alarm spiralled in volume, its sound chilling him. A flash from the house had him wheeling again, searching for the epicentre. It was the Manse itself.

Detonation after detonation rocked the building, flame slashed through the roof, explosions thundered, the walls rippled, great sections sucking inwards with stunning power. Windows shattered, their glass flying inside, roof supports collapsed and fell, tiles showered into the upper floor which buckled under the weight of new explosions. A thudding sound came again and again, the impact of falling rock sending a cloud of dust into the sky, forcing him to come lower and to the side of the Manse.

Even there, he could see very little but the flame guttering in the daylight gloom. Fire washed left and right, wood cracked and splintered, the entire south wall fell as if some giant hand had shoved it from the outside. It was mesmerising.

Arteche shook his head, a mana-led wind buffeting him as the wards savaged the Septern Manse, reducing to broken timber, ash and rubble, the life of Balaia's greatest ever, yet fatally flawed mage.

'Septern, Septern, what have you done?'

The wind blew away the dust, revealing an inferno chasing through what remained of the ground floor. Charred stone cracked in the heat, wood burned so fiercely the flame looked blood red, and in the fire, Arteche could see the end of a treasure trove of work as pages flew in the updraft to be snatched by the flame and consumed in an instant.

There was no sense in looking for survivors and the ageing

Dordovan master turned a tired circle and flew away. He passed the Wesmen lines, saw them pointing as they peered through the illusions and heard the cheer echoing through the camp. No doubt they would charge in again, not realising that the wards covering the grounds would remain active long after the ruin had chilled, some for years.

'Primitives,' he muttered. 'None of us has victory today.'

He increased his speed and flew to his army, a more palatable version of the events he had just witnessed already forming in his mind. This would all have to be handled very, very carefully.

)(

The dark was comforting for Septern. He had found a wall against which to lie, imagining in his mind, the devastation he had unleashed above. He searched for sorrow at the lives he had taken but could find none, his only regret being the loss of so much work. It was fortunate he had been so diligent in taking vital copy documents to the colleges. He would have hated nothing more than for his life to have been wasted.

He was cold and the blood still flowed from his chest. There was no going back now. If he were to survive, he had to travel the rips to Beshara, the dragon dimension. But it seemed such a long way. Two painful transfers and a dusty plateau. At least he could see his niece again.

He smiled to himself, drew in a rattling breath and settled back against the wall. It was strangely comfortable and the utter dark sought to warm him in its embrace. Perhaps he would stay here a little while, get his strength back. The blood would stop soon and he could tie something round the wound.

Not a bad idea. An extreme exhaustion was upon him and he wasn't at all sure if he could walk to the rip, whose pale luminescence was just edging into his eyes now he was adjusting to the dark. He tucked the amulet back into his blood soaked shirt and let his head drop to his chest.

He had beaten the Wytch Lords and he had beaten the colleges. Not bad for a morning's work, not bad at all. They would be writing about that for decades to come. The name of Septern would surely go down in history now for more than his magical genius. He had saved Balaia. He only hoped they fully understood that.

Septern closed his eyes and let the darkness take its hold. Just a short rest, then. Just a short one. Short.

# OTHER
# TITLES FROM
# PS PUBLISHING

*Winner of the British Fantasy Award*
*2001 & 2002*

Please order direct from:
PS PUBLISHING LLP
HAMILTON HOUSE
4 PARK AVENUE
HARROGATE
HG2 9BQ
ENGLAND

or via the website
http://www.pspublishing.co.uk

or by e-mailing
crowth1@attglobal.net

Add £2 or $5 for first class/airmail postage for the first book;
add £1 or $3 for each additional book.
PayPal and most major credit cards accepted.
Please make sterling cheques payable to PS Publishing;
make $US checks payable to Peter Crowther

# LENINGRAD NIGHTS
A novella by Graham Joyce
Introduction by Peter Straub
Hardcover (52 copies) — SOLD OUT     Paperback — SOLD OUT

# HOW THE OTHER HALF LIVES
A novella by James Lovegrove
Introduction by Colin Greenland
Hardcover (52 copies) — SOLD OUT     Paperback — £8/$14

# ANDY WARHOL'S DRACULA
A novella by Kim Newman
Introduction by F. Paul Wilson
Hardcover (125 copies) — SOLD OUT     Paperback — SOLD OUT

# THE VACCINATOR
A novella by Michael Marshall Smith
Introduction by M. John Harrison
Hardcover (150 copies) — SOLD OUT     Paperback — SOLD OUT

# REALITY DUST
A novella by Stephen Baxter
Introduction by Greg Bear
Hardcover (300 copies) — SOLD OUT     Paperback — SOLD OUT

# WATCHING TREES GROW
A novella by Peter F. Hamilton
Introduction by Larry Niven
Hardcover (300 copies) — SOLD OUT     Paperback — SOLD OUT

# TENDELEO'S STORY
(Winner of the Theodore Sturgeon Award, 2001)
A novella by Ian McDonald
Introduction by Robert Silverberg
Hardcover (300 copies) — £25/$40          Paperback — £8/$14

# MAKING HISTORY
A novella by Paul J. McAuley
Introduction by Michael Swanwick
Hardcover (200 copies) — SOLD OUT   Paperback —SOLD OUT

# NAMING OF PARTS
(Winner of the British Fantasy Award, 2001)
A novella by Tim Lebbon
Introduction by Steve Rasnic Tem
Hardcover (300 copies) — SOLD OUT    Paperback — £8/$14

# A WRITER'S LIFE
A novella by Eric Brown
Introduction by Paul Di Filippo
Hardcover (300 copies) — £25/$40          Paperback — £8/$14

# NEARLY PEOPLE
A novella by Conrad Williams
Introduction by Michael Marshall Smith
Hardcover (300 copies) — £25/$40          Paperback — £8/$14

# THE ASTONISHED EYE
A novel by Tracy Knight
Introduction by Philip José Farmer
Slipcased hardcover (26 copies) — SOLD OUT
Hardcover (500 copies) — SOLD OUT

# DIAMOND DOGS

A novella by Alastair Reynolds
Introduction by Stephen Baxter
Hardcover (400 copies) — SOLD OUT    Paperback — SOLD OUT

# INFINITY PLUS ONE

A 110,000-word anthology edited by Keith Brooke and Nick Gevers
Stories by Michael Bishop, Tony Daniel, Paul Di Filippo, Mary
Gentle, James Patrick Kelly, Garry Kilworth, Ian MacLeod, Kim
Newman, Patrick O'Leary, Kit Reed, Kim Stanley Robinson, Michael
Swanwick and Jeff VanderMeer
Introduction by Peter F. Hamilton
Hardcover (500 copies) — SOLD OUT

# PARK POLAR

A novella by Adam Roberts
Introduction by Roger Levy
Hardcover (400 copies) — £25/$40        Paperback — £8/$14

# THE HUMAN FRONT

(Winner of the Sidewise Award for Alternate History, 2001)
A novella by Ken MacLeod
Introduction by Iain M. Banks
Hardcover (400 copies)  — SOLD OUT  Paperback — SOLD OUT

# THE DARKEST PART OF THE WOODS

Ramsey Campbell's first full-length supernatural novel for four years
Introduction by Peter Straub
Slipcased hardcover (100 copies) — £55/$80
Hardcover (500 copies) — £35/$55

## A YEAR IN THE LINEAR CITY

A novella by Paul Di Filippo
Introduction by Michael Bishop
Hardcover (300 copies) — £25/$40        Paperback — £8/$14

## BLOOD FOLLOWS

By Steven Erikson — the first in a projected cycle of novella-length
stories featuring Bauchelain and Korbal Broach
Introduction by Stephen Donaldson
Hardcover (300 copies) — SOLD OUT   Paperback — SOLD OUT

## THE UGLIMEN

A short novel by Mark Morris
Introduction by Stephen Laws
Hardcover (300 copies) — £25/$40        Paperback — £8/$14

## THE FAIRY FELLER'S MASTER STROKE

A novella by Mark Chadbourn
Introduction by Neil Gaiman
Hardcover (300 copies) — £25/$40        Paperback — £8/$14

## V.A.O.

A novella by Geoff Ryman
Introduction by Gwyneth Jones
Hardcover (300 copies) — £25/$40        Paperback — £8/$14

## FIRING THE CATHEDRAL

A new Jerry Cornelius novella by Michael Moorcock
Introduction by Alan Moore
Hardcover (400 copies) — £25/$40        Paperback — £8/$14

# KEEP OUT THE NIGHT

An anthology edited and introduced by Stephen Jones, in the great tradition of Christine Campbell Thompson's acclaimed *Not At Night* series.
Stories by Sydney J. Bounds, Poppy Z. Brite, Ramsey Campbell, Hugh B. Cave, Basil Copper, Dennis Etchison, Neil Gaiman, Caitlin R. Kiernan, Tim Lebbon, Brian Lumley, Kim Newman and Michael Marshall Smith.
Interior illustrations by Randy Broecker.
Hardcover (500 copies, signed by the Editor) — £45/$65
Slipcased hardcover (100 copies, signed by all contributors) — £65/$90

# RIDING THE ROCK

A novella by Stephen Baxter
Introduction by Gregory Benford
Hardcover (400 copies) — £25/$40      Paperback — £8/$14

# RAMSEY CAMPBELL, PROBABLY

A 140,000-word collection of articles and essays written over the past three decades by Ramsey Campbell.
Edited by S.T. Joshi
Introduction by Douglas E. Winter
Cover (and slipcased edition interior artwork) by J. K. Potter
Trade paperback (500 copies) — £30/$45
Slipcased hardcover (100 copies) — £65/$90

# JUPITER MAGNIFIED

A novella by Adam Roberts
Introduction by James Lovegrove
Hardcover (400 copies) — £25/$40      Paperback — £8/$14

## THE TAIN
A novella by China Miéville
Introduction by M. John Harrison
Hardcover (400 copies) — £25/$40          Paperback — £8/$14

## WHITE BIZANGO
A novella by Stephen Gallagher
Introduction by Joe R. Lansdale
Hardcover (400 copies) — £25/$40          Paperback — £8/$14

## LIGHT STEALER
A novella by James Barclay
Introduction by Stan Nicholls
Hardcover (300 copies) — £25/$40          Paperback — £8/$14

## RIGHTEOUS BLOOD
A double novella by Cliff Burns
Introduction by Tim Lebbon
Hardcover (300 copies) — £25/$40          Paperback — £8/$14

## IN SPRINGDALE TOWN
A novella by Robert Freeman Wexler
Introduction by Lucius Shepard
Hardcover (300 copies) — £25/$40          Paperback — £8/$14

# COMING SOON

## JIGSAW MEN
A novella by Gary Greenwood
Introduction to be confirmed
Hardcover (300 copies) — £25/$40      Paperback — £8/$14


## INFINITY PLUS TWO
An anthology edited by Keith Brooke and Nick Gevers
Stories by Stephen Baxter, Terry Bisson, Eric Brown, Lisa Goldstein,
Paul McAuley, Ian McDonald, Vonda McIntyre, Michael Moorcock,
Paul Park, Adam Roberts, Lucius Shepard, Brian Stableford and
Charles Stross
Introduction by John Clute
Hardcover (500 copies) — £45/$65


## THE HEALTHY DEAD
Following on from the popular BLOOD FOLLOWS, Steven Erikson
delivers the second in the cycle of novella-length stories featuring
Bauchelain and Korbal Broach
Introduction to be confirmed
Hardcover (400 copies) — £25/$40      Paperback — £8/$14


## CHANGING OF FACES
A novella by Tim Lebbon
Introduction to be confirmed
Hardcover (300 copies) — £25/$40      Paperback — £8/$14

# FUZZY DICE

A novel by Paul Di Filippo
Introduction by Rudy Rucker
Slipcased hardcover (200 copies) — £55/$80
Hardcover (500 copies) — £35/$55